# Stephanie Meets Mr. Perfect

Am I dreaming? she wondered. Or is it really him?

Stay calm, Stephanie told herself. Take a close look, but stay calm!

It was him!

Zack!

The famous lead singer of Zack and the Zees!

She couldn't believe it. Zack. Right here at the Galaxy Grill. Sitting there . . . looking at her!

Zack's eyes darted to either side. He pulled his cap lower to hide more of his face. "Please don't give me away," he whispered. "I just sneaked in for some food. I didn't know that this place would be so mobbed."

He smiled at her, slid off his stool, and sneaked out of the diner.

Stephanie turned slowly around to find her newest friend, Brandi, standing behind her. Stephanie grabbed her arm. "You know him?" she whispered. "You actually know Zack?"

Brandi grinned. "You're not excited or anything, are you?"

"Who wouldn't be?" Stephanie answered.

Brandi smiled at her. "You know, we're having a barbecue on my dad's yacht tomorrow afternoon. Zack will be there. Would you like to come along?"

"Are you kidding? Yes!" Stephanie grabbed the table to keep from floating up to the ceiling. She'd just entered total heaven!

Zack wasn't just a handsome face on a CD cover anymore. He was someone she'd actually met. And tomorrow, she was going to a party with him.

She was going to a party with her perfect guy!

**FULL HOUSE™: Stephanie novels**

Available from MINSTREL Books

# Full House™

# Club Stephanie

## Friend or Flamingo?

**Based on the hit Warner Bros.
TV series**

**Wendy Haley**

A Parachute Book

READING

A
MINSTREL®
BOOK

Published by POCKET BOOKS
New York   London   Toronto   Sydney   Tokyo   Singapore

9934357

A MINSTREL PAPERBACK *ORIGINAL*

 POCKET BOOKS, a division of Simon & Schuster Inc. 1230 Avenue of the Americas, New York, NY 10020

A PARACHUTE BOOK

 Copyright © and ™ 1998 by Warner Bros.

FULL HOUSE, characters, names and all related indicia are trademarks of Warner Bros. © 1998.

ISBN: 0-671-02123-0

First Minstrel Books printing July 1998

10  9  8  7  6  5  4  3  2  1

A MINSTREL BOOK and colophon are registered trademarks of Simon & Schuster Inc.

FULL HOUSE, characters, names and all related indicia are trademarks of Lorimar Television © 1998.

Cover photo by Schultz Photography

Printed in the U.S.A.

# Friend or Flamingo?

# CHAPTER
# 1

♦ ◄ ◗ ♦

"I can't wait till we all start Summer Sail again," Stephanie Tanner declared. "Maybe this time I'll meet the perfect guy. Maybe we all will. Right?" she asked. "Hello? Anyone?"

Stephanie leaped off her bike and scanned the parking lot of the yacht club. The wind whipping off San Francisco Bay blew her long, blond hair into her face. She brushed it back as she searched for her friends.

They were riding a little way behind her. No, she realized, a long way behind her. They were just making the turn into the lot, talking a mile a minute. All four of them.

Darcy Powell, Allie Taylor, Kayla Norris, and Anna Rice didn't seem to notice they were lagging behind. Stephanie grinned. It was hard to believe that the five of them hadn't been best friends forever.

Stephanie, Allie, and Darcy were already best friends when they met Anna and Kayla the past summer. In no time they were doing everything together. They had even run their own summer camp for little kids.

This summer, they all joined Summer Sail—a program that taught teens everything about sailing. Summer Sail ran in three sessions—one for each month of summer. The June session had been a total blast.

Stephanie locked her bike in the rack and waited for the others to join her. "What's with you guys?" she asked. "Are you *trying* to be late?"

"Not a chance," Darcy replied. "Not after you called every one of us at the crack of dawn to make sure we'd be up early."

"Can you blame me?" Stephanie asked. "Look around. How could you miss one minute of this?"

Stephanie thought the yacht club at the marina was one of the prettiest places in San Francisco. A wide green lawn stretched from the edge of the parking lot down to the water. The large white clubhouse sat in the middle of the lawn, surrounded by flowers in dazzling colors. It looked especially striking against the backdrop of deep blue water.

Boats rocked gently in their slips set along the long wooden docks. A forest of masts showed where the smaller sailboats were docked. It seemed as if there were hundreds of them.

"I hope there's a sailboat left for us," Darcy joked as she scanned the docks. Darcy was tall, with smooth brown skin, a dazzling smile, and an awesome sense of humor.

"Okay, so we're here a little early," Stephanie said. "It's better than being late for the first day of the July session."

"I guess that's true," Allie agreed with a good-natured smile. Allie was always good-natured. It was one of the things Stephanie liked most about her. They had been best friends since their first day of kindergarten. They were fourteen now—Stephanie guessed they both had to be really good-natured to get along so well for that long!

Darcy and the others locked their bikes into the bike rack. Anna fastened a barrette into her wiry, dark curls. It was almost impossible for her to keep her hair in place in the strong winds that always swept through the marina. Her freckled face lit up with a smile as she spotted a curly-haired blond boy steering his green car into the parking lot.

"Hey—there's Josh. Josh, over here!" Anna called.

Josh Hogan was seventeen and an assistant sailing instructor for Summer Sail. He spotted Anna, and his wide, friendly grin spread even wider.

"Anna, don't call him over," Kayla whispered. "Stephanie might be embarrassed."

"No way," Stephanie said. "I got over my crush on Josh a long time ago."

"You and Darah Judson," Darcy teased. "I hope that's the last time you and she ever go after the same boy!"

Stephanie and Darah had fought over Josh for most of June. In the end they found out that he already had a girlfriend, one his own age. He wasn't interested in either one of them!

"Did you have to bring up Darah—and the Flamingoes?" Kayla leaned against Anna and groaned, making a face as if she'd just bit into a lemon. A very sour lemon.

The Flamingoes were a snobby group of girls. They were rich and pretty and really, really popular—though Stephanie found it hard to believe that people didn't see right through them.

Sure, the Flamingoes always looked great.

They acted friendly enough, too. But they would do anything to stay popular, which included acting mean and nasty.

The Flamingoes were Stephanie's worst enemies. They were always playing dirty tricks on her and her friends. Darah Judson was the meanest and nastiest of them all.

"That's who we were talking about riding over here," Anna told Stephanie. "The Flamingoes! Kayla doesn't believe they're coming back this month."

"Why would they?" Kayla asked. "Summer Sail is fun, but it's also hard work. And they hate work!"

"Yeah, but their families are important members of the yacht club," Stephanie pointed out. "They'll probably make them come back."

"Great. They're going to act like spoiled brats again." Darcy's voice rose in a perfect imitation of Darah's whine. "Ooooh, I can't haul in the line—I broke a nail! And those white sails don't go with my new pink bikini!"

Kayla, Anna, and Allie burst out laughing, but Stephanie covered her ears. "I don't want to hear any more about the Flamingoes," she declared. "Tons of new kids signed up for this session, and you know what that means. . . ."

5

"Another chance to find the perfect guy!" Allie exclaimed.

"Don't start that again," Anna warned.

"What?" Stephanie pretended to look offended. "Are you against us finding the perfect guy?"

Before Summer Sail even began, all five friends had decided that this summer would be different. They were fourteen now and aching to find guys for themselves. Not just any guy. *The* guy. The perfect guy!

"You know Anna doesn't believe the perfect guy exists," Kayla remarked.

"That's crazy," Stephanie replied. "There's a perfect match for everyone. You just have to find him."

"Maybe," Anna said. "But you won't find him by deciding you *have* to. You'll just meet him one day."

"But that leaves everything to chance!" Allie protested.

"Allie's right," Stephanie said. "You have to look for your Mr. Perfect."

"Well, good luck finding him around here." Anna shook her head as they crossed the walkway that led past the clubhouse and out along the docks.

6

"Wow! Would you look at that!" Darcy pointed to a huge yacht docked at the end slip.

Stephanie felt her mouth drop open. "What is it? A boat or a floating hotel?"

"I have never, ever seen such a fancy boat," Kayla declared.

"It even has its own swimming pool!" Anna gaped at the lower deck, where the pool shimmered like a bright blue jewel.

"And its own helicopter!" Allie pointed to the top deck, where a gleaming helicopter waited.

Stephanie shaded her eyes to stare at the yacht. "Who do you think owns a boat like that?"

"Someone rich," Anna cracked.

"That's obvious," Darcy said. "Wouldn't it be cool if it belonged to a famous athlete? They could discover me, and I could be a famous athlete!"

"You *are* an athlete, Darce," Stephanie agreed. "But I don't think knowing someone famous is how any of us will get famous. I bet Anna wants it to belong to a famous artist who can discover that *Anna's* a fabulous artist—and buy all her drawings and stuff, right?"

"Sounds good to me," Anna answered.

"No way!" Kayla raised her clasped hands to the sky. "Please, let it belong to Will Jones!"

"Oh, you and Will Jones! Ever since we saw his lastest movie, he's all you can talk about!" Anna gave her a friendly shove.

"Wouldn't it be incredible if he *did* own that yacht?" Kayla asked in a dreamy voice. "And we all got to meet him?"

"Yes, but I wouldn't count on it happening," Stephanie told her.

"Hey, look!" Darcy jabbed Stephanie with an elbow and pointed at the yacht. "I saw someone moving past the window. Maybe it's Will!"

Stephanie laughed. "You're kidding, right?"

"Well, the someone was wearing jeans and a tank top and looked pretty cool," Darcy replied.

Stephanie stared more closely at the yacht. She saw a slim figure striding toward the gangplank. "You're right!" she said. "Someone is there! And is headed right this way!"

# CHAPTER

# 2

◆ ◀ ◗ ◆

The slim figure drew closer.

"Oh," Stephanie said in disappointment. "That's definitely not my perfect guy."

"But she may be a perfect girl," Darcy teased.

The person crossing the gangplank was a slim girl about their own age. She wore flare-leg jeans with roses embroidered along each leg and a funky-looking tank top made of hundreds of tiny fabric squares sewn together. Her shoulder-length hair gleamed red-brown in the sun.

She stopped for a moment and Stephanie saw that she was staring at the dock where the *Sunshine* rocked gently in her slip.

The schooner *Sunshine* was large—two hundred feet from stem to stern. When the sails on her two tall masts were filled with air, she looked like a giant white bird with wings spread for flight.

The *Sunshine* was also headquarters for Summer Sail kids. They had meetings and sailing lessons on her wide deck every day.

Stephanie saw the slim girl square her shoulders as she headed up the gangplank of the *Sunshine*. Stephanie thought she appeared to be nervous.

"I wonder who she is," she said.

"Oh—look who's here! Our favorite people!"

Stephanie slowly turned around—and groaned. The Flamingoes were hurrying down the dock, heading her way. Darah led the pack, followed by Tiffany Schroeder, Mary Kelly, and Cynthia Hanson.

"Flamingo alert," Stephanie warned in a whisper.

Tiffany stopped to run a hand through her blond hair, showing off a set of pale blue nails. Stephanie saw that they were decorated with tiny pink flamingoes.

"Well, look who's here," Tiffany said, gazing at Stephanie.

"I didn't expect to see any of you here again!" Darah exclaimed.

Darah looked great, as always. She wore tight

white shorts and a turquoise crop top that showed off her perfect tan. Her hair was pulled back in a perfect French braid. Even her makeup was perfect.

Stephanie suddenly felt as if her new purple shorts outfit wasn't special at all. *That's silly*, she told herself. *Don't let Darah get to you.*

Josh appeared on the dock with Ryan Black and Jenny Burton, the other sailing instructors, and Craig Walter. Craig was in charge of the Summer Sail program. He graduated from college the year before and trained all the instructors. Sometimes Craig also taught classes.

Josh, Ryan, and Jenny nodded hellos as they passed the girls. Craig paused. "Shouldn't you be getting on board?" he asked.

"We're right behind you," Darah said. "We can't wait to get started!" She shot Tiffany an excited smile as they moved up the gangplank. Cynthia and Mary giggled.

*What are they all grinning about?* Stephanie wondered.

"There she is!" Tiffany gasped, pointing to the girl from the yacht. She was standing on the deck of the *Sunshine*.

"There *who* is?" Stephanie asked.

Craig caught sight of her and walked over to

greet her. "Brandi!" he exclaimed. "Glad you could make it."

"Yeah. Well . . ." Brandi muttered.

"Hi! I'm Darah Judson, and these are my friends." Darah and the Flamingoes crowded around Brandi, fighting to get close to her.

Stephanie exchanged bewildered looks with Darcy, Allie, Kayla, and Anna as they stepped on board. "Who is Brandi?" she asked.

"This is Brandi Gardner," Craig said, introducing her. "Her father, Steve Gardner, is the head of Penny Ault Records."

"Steve Gardner, the record producer?" Stephanie gaped at Brandi in astonishment. "Didn't your dad just sign Zack and the Zees to a big recording contract?"

"Yeah, he did," Brandi replied.

Stephanie glanced at Darcy. She could tell they were thinking the same thing: Brandi was the reason the Flamingoes showed up for Summer Sail again!

Somehow they had found out that Brandi would be there. They were planning to make friends with her—the way they tried to make friends with anyone who was cool, or rich, or glamorous.

Stephanie and her friends were shoved from

12

behind as the *Sunshine* filled with more boys and girls. There were about thirty of them altogether.

Craig raised his voice to be heard over their noise. "Listen up, people!" he called. "For those of you who are new, welcome aboard! You're going to be very busy in the next few weeks. You'll have sailing instruction every day, and spend a few hours on the water practicing what Josh, Jenny, Ryan, and I teach you." Craig paused. "But besides sailing, there's a very special event this month. Flotilla Week."

"What is a flotilla, anyway?" Kayla asked.

Someone behind her snickered as Craig nodded at her. "Good question," he told her. "A flotilla is a parade on the water—a parade of floats. You will form teams and each team will build its own float. Then we parade them in the shallow part of the marina."

"Are the floats like the ones in the Tournament of Roses parade?" a curly-haired boy called out. "Those are huge!"

"Don't worry," Craig assured him. "Your floats will be much smaller than that. They're actually rowboats. Each team gets a rowboat to decorate any way you want. You can put things in the boats, or make a platform that rests on top of the boat. You can ride in them, or not.

13

Here, these pictures will make everything more clear."

Craig pulled a package of photographs from the back pocket of his shorts. "These pictures are of winning floats from other years. They'll show what you can do with a little hard work and a lot of imagination."

Stephanie and her friends waited impatiently until it was their turn to see the photographs. They showed all kinds of crazy ideas.

One photo showed a giant Mexican sombrero built on a platform rising above the boat. An enormous prickly cactus sat on each side of the hat, and the figure of a black cat was suspended above it all.

The cat must have been hanging from wires, to make it look as if it were caught in midflight. The cat seemed to be yowling with pain.

"He looks like he just sat on a cactus—and it hurt!" Allie said.

Another photo was of a boat carrying a fat, jolly snowman surrounded by reindeer and glittering snowflakes. The name of the float, "Christmas in July," was scrawled across the back of the photo.

Another float featured a giant peacock sitting in the rowboat, its incredible tail feathers spread out around it and trailing into the water. Craig

14

told them that the peacock's "feathers" were actually made of recycled plastic bags.

"That's amazing!" Anna exclaimed.

"What are the rest of the floats made from?" Stephanie asked.

"Anything and everything," Craig answered. "Bottles, cans, cotton balls—you name it. On Flotilla Night, all the floats are towed across the bay in a parade. Judges will award a trophy to the best float, and the winning team will be on local TV and in the newspapers," he added.

"The Flamingoes have got to win that trophy!" Darah's voice rang out in the crowd.

# CHAPTER
# 3

◆ ◀ ◢ ◆

Stephanie felt a burst of anger. Darah always had to win first prize in everything—whether she deserved it or not!

Craig laughed. "Hold on. There's more, Darah," he said. "The winners will also get free tickets to see Zack and the Zees in concert! With backstage passes to meet them in person."

Stephanie screamed. She couldn't help it. She wasn't the only one. Allie grabbed her hands and they both jumped up and down in excitement.

"Steph, you could meet Zack!" Allie squealed. "It'd be a dream come true."

Craig held up his hands for quiet again. He sought out Brandi in the crowd.

"We want to thank Brandi and her father,"

Craig went on. "They donated the Zack and the Zees tickets."

Cheers and applause rang out. Brandi blushed.

Stephanie saw Darah elbow a few kids aside so she could stand next to Brandi. She threw an arm around Brandi's shoulders.

"That is so cool of your dad!" Darah announced. "I bet you've met Zack hundreds of times, right?"

Brandi's cheeks got even redder.

*Darah is embarrassing her!* Stephanie realized. She felt bad for Brandi. She might be the daughter of a big-time record producer, but she was also new to Summer Sail. She didn't know anyone there, and the way Darah was gushing over her obviously made her feel self-conscious.

Stephanie suddenly caught Brandi's gaze. Stephanie shrugged as if to say, "Just ignore Darah." Brandi appeared surprised for a moment. Then she ducked her head and giggled.

The crowd shifted and Brandi pulled away from Darah. Stephanie glanced at her from the corner of her eye.

*What do you say to somebody whose dad runs a record company?* she wondered. Everyone probably made a big fuss over Brandi and asked if she knew any celebrities.

Brandi stared down at her feet. She looked as

17

if she wanted to be anywhere but in a crowd of noisy strangers.

Stephanie walked over to her. "So, why are you at Summer Sail, anyway?" she blurted out.

Brandi seemed surprised again. "Good question!" she replied. "I mean, I don't know how to sail at all. We usually live in New York, but my dad came here for an important record deal. He thought I should do something fun while we're here."

"Your dad sounds like a nice guy, to worry about you like that," Stephanie remarked.

"Yeah. Well, we always try to spend part of my summer vacation together," Brandi explained. "He works too hard to spend a lot of time with me the rest of the year. And we're really close. I know that sounds lame," she added.

"Not to me," Stephanie said. "I'm close to my dad, too. And my other two 'dads.' "

"Huh?" Brandi looked confused. Stephanie explained about how her mother died when she was little. And how her dad asked her uncle Jesse and his friend Joey to help raise Stephanie, her older sister, D.J., and her little sister, Michelle.

"Then Jesse got married. And he and my aunt Becky had twin boys," Stephanie went on. "So

18

now nine people live in my house. Plus Comet, our dog. It gets crazy sometimes, but it's kind of fun, too."

"It sounds like lots of fun." Brandi's eyes sparkled. "My parents are divorced, and I don't have any brothers or sisters. I'd love to see a big family like that in action."

"Maybe you could meet them sometime," Stephanie offered.

"Really? That would be so cool!" Brandi said.

*Brandi seems like a regular person*, Stephanie thought. *I like her.*

She glanced down and noticed the watch Brandi wore. "Hey, your watch stopped," she said.

"Oh, it isn't real," Brandi said. "It's a fake tattoo. I painted it on my skin."

Stephanie stared. "That's amazing! Can I see?"

Brandi held her arm out and Stephanie studied the watch. Every tiny detail was carefully painted, including the glints of light that would have shone on the glass of a real watch case.

"Incredible," Stephanie murmured. "You even made the watchband look like real leather! What a fantastic job."

"Thanks," Brandi said, obviously pleased.

"You know, Anna is the artistic one in our

group," Stephanie told her. "You have got to show her this. She'll love it!"

"Don't make a fuss," Brandi said. "I just like painting stuff. Once, I painted a climbing rose on my friend's leg. It looked so real that her parents grounded her for getting a tattoo without permission!"

"No way!" Stephanie burst out laughing. "Seriously, Brandi, you have got to work on our float. Would you be on our team?"

"Oh. I don't know. I—" Brandi stopped when Anna and Darcy appeared.

"Steph! Craig is handing out pieces of paper so we can make a list of the names on our float team," Anna announced.

Before Stephanie could say anything, Brandi disappeared in the crowd. Allie and Kayla joined her.

"I wanted you to meet Brandi," Stephanie told her friends. "She seems really nice. Plus, she's a really good artist. I definitely think she should work on our float."

"Really?" Kayla asked.

"Why not?" Stephanie replied. "She doesn't know anybody else here."

"I have an even better idea," Anna said. "Let's ask her to come out to dinner with us tonight. Then we can all get to know her better."

"Especially if she's going to work with us," Allie added.

"Don't worry. You'll love her," Stephanie said. As they pushed through the crowd, they talked about what kind of float they might make.

"There she is." Stephanie pointed out Brandi, who was standing by the main mast. They rushed up to her.

"Brandi!" Stephanie called. "Would you like to hang with me and my friends tonight?" she asked. "We planned something really special for the first night after the new session of Summer Sail."

"Right," Allie added. "We're going to the Galaxy Grill. We've never been there, but it's supposed to be the hottest new place in town."

Brandi nodded. "That's what I heard. I'd like to go with you, but I told these other girls I'd go out with them tonight."

"Oh." Stephanie felt a burst of disappointment. "Well, maybe we could all hang out together. Who are you going with?"

"Them." To Stephanie's horror, Brandi gestured toward the Flamingoes. "I'm going with Darah and Tiffany!"

21

# CHAPTER
# 4

◆ ◀ ▪ ◆

"How do I look?" Stephanie paused outside the entrance to the Galaxy Grill.

Allie took her in from head to toe. Stephanie wore white stretchy pants and a lavender and green striped shirt.

"You look fantastic," Allie said. "In fact, I think we all do."

Allie and Kayla had on cutoffs with bright-colored crop tops and cardigans tied at their waists. Anna wore her usual "funky" outfit—wide red pants with a white T-shirt and a green embroidered vest. Darcy was in jeans and a halter top.

"We do look fantastic," Stephanie replied. "And that's good—because I'm ready to party!"

"Me, too," Darcy agreed.

The Galaxy was an enormous diner made of shiny silver metal. A bright green neon sign flashed GALAXY GRILL over and over.

Stephanie pushed the front door open and was greeted by a blast of music so loud she could feel it throbbing through the soles of her shoes.

Kayla pinched her excitedly. "This place is so cool!"

Neon stars glowed in patterns across the ceiling, which was also painted to show the planets. Some of the booths were designed to look like planets, too.

Saturn and Jupiter were the most popular booths because they were decorated with glowing neon rings that surrounded the people inside with pulsing bands of blue, gold, and red.

Every booth was packed. Kids yelled back and forth from one side of the place to the other. The waiters and waitresses had to hold their trays over their heads, weaving around the people who were dancing in the aisles.

"Look!" Darcy exclaimed. "Those kids are leaving. Grab that booth before somebody else gets it!"

Stephanie and Darcy raced toward the booth. Stephanie dove across one seat as Kayla, Allie, and Anna slid into the other side.

"Safe!" Anna called as if they were at a baseball game.

Darcy leaned out into the aisle. "Wow! Steph, check out that guy two tables away. He's a dead ringer for Zack."

"No way. Where?" Stephanie craned her neck for a better look. "You're crazy, Darce," she said. "He doesn't look a thing like Zack. Zack is tons cuter."

"You mean, *this* Zack?" Kayla teased as she whipped a copy of *Teen Dream* out of her backpack. She flipped it open to a long article on Zack and the Zees.

"Let me see Zack's pictures!" Stephanie grabbed the magazine and stared. Zack had intense blue eyes and dark eyebrows. He wore jeans, a black shirt, and a beat-up leather jacket.

"He is so cute!" Stephanie sighed. "And he just turned seventeen—the perfect age. The perfect everything." She stared at his picture. "Oh, look—he has a tiny scar near his right eye. I never knew that."

"I suppose the scar is perfect, too," Darcy teased.

"Totally," Stephanie replied.

"I wonder what it would be like to meet him?" Allie asked.

"Totally awesome," Stephanie replied.

They ordered and watched the crowd while they waited for their food. "Do you see Brandi here anywhere?" Stephanie asked. "I was hoping we could catch her alone for a minute—so I could ask her to be on our float team."

Anna looked annoyed. "I thought she was coming with the Flamingoes."

"She is," Stephanie admitted. "But I decided not to hold that against her. Brandi doesn't know anyone around here. She probably just wants to make friends. And the Flamingoes look cool and hip."

"It's true—she doesn't know how rotten the Flamingoes can be," Allie added.

"Right," Stephanie agreed. "Believe me, we want her on our team. She is one great artist."

"Well, Anna and I already had a couple of ideas for our float," Kayla said, giving Anna a quick glance. "How about a tropical island?"

Stephanie shook her head. "That's probably been done a million times. What about mermaids?"

Allie made a face. "That's probably been done more than tropical islands."

"How about a whale?" Anna said. "Everybody likes whales, and we could do something cool with the blowhole."

"That's a great idea," Kayla said.

"I like it, too," Allie agreed.

"It could be fun," Darcy added.

"Maybe," Stephanie said. "Let's think some more."

The front door swung open. The Flamingoes came strutting in. Darah led the way, with Tiffany sticking close beside her. They wore leather miniskirts and denim jean jackets. Cynthia and Tina had on tank dresses with sweaters tied around their shoulders.

A few boys nearby stopped talking to stare at them. So did some of the girls.

Stephanie was relieved to see that Brandi wasn't with them. Darah pointed to a booth that some kids were just leaving. Another group of kids was waiting for it to empty out. They were about to sit down, when Darah strode up to the table and sat in the booth.

One girl who had been waiting frowned and slid onto the seat across from her. The tabletop was still cluttered with plates and half-full glasses of soda. Stephanie saw Darah casually sweep her arm across the table, pretending to shove a glass aside. It tipped over—spilling sticky, dark cola all over the girl's white shorts.

The girl leaped up in surprise. She stared at the soda stain in shock. Stephanie saw Darah shake her head as if she were feeling sorry for the girl. Tiffany actually handed her a handful of napkins! Then the rest of the Flamingoes slid past her to get into the booth.

The girl shot them an angry look before stomping off to clean her shorts in the ladies' room. Her friends went with her, giving the Flamingoes more dirty looks. Darah flashed them a phony smile—as if she didn't know what she'd done.

*Typical Flamingoes,* Stephanie thought. *Brandi wouldn't like Darah if she saw her act that way, would she?*

"Hey, you guys!" a familiar voice called.

"Hi, Josh!" Stephanie waved him over.

Josh slid into the booth next to Kayla and Allie. "It's so great that you guys are all back this session," he told them. "The flotilla is going to be fantastic."

Darah spotted Josh and hurried over to their booth. "Hey, Josh!" She flashed him a flirty smile. "Come over to my booth. We were just going to talk about our float. I bet you could give us tons of pointers."

"Sorry, Darah," Josh said. "I can't play favorites. You guys all have to work on your own."

He glanced at his watch. "I'd better head out," he told them. "I've got to be up extra early tomorrow. See you at the marina."

Darah stared after him, obviously disappointed.

"What are you doing?" Anna asked Darah. "We all know Josh has a totally gorgeous, totally nice girlfriend. Why waste your time trying to get him interested in you?"

Darah scowled at her in disgust. "Guys are always interested in me," she snapped. "I'm a Flamingo. And I never waste my time! I'm not a loser, like *some* people I know."

Anna watched her with a calm expression. "You're wasting your time if you think the Flamingoes will win the flotilla trophy," she said.

Darah scowled. "Oh, we'll win, all right. So don't waste too much time on your little project. You won't have a chance."

"You are so wrong," Stephanie told her. "We'll win. We'll be in the papers and on TV. Our float is going to be awesome."

"Don't count on it," Darah said. "Our float will make yours look like a kindergarten project. Those concert tickets are as good as ours! We're going to meet Zack and the Zees. And once they meet us, they'll love us!"

Darah spun on her heel and marched back to her booth.

"She makes me so mad!" Stephanie exploded.

"She just wants those tickets because she knows how much I want them!"

The front door opened again and Stephanie saw Brandi step inside. She pulled back as the blast of music hit her. She was dressed all in black, which made her reddish-brown hair look redder than ever.

"There's Brandi!" Stephanie exclaimed. She started to get up and wave.

"Over here, Brandi!" Tiffany yelled from the Flamingoes' booth. Brandi walked over to them and dropped her bag on the table.

"So much for getting to Brandi first," Stephanie murmured.

Brandi shrugged off her black jean jacket. As she reached to hang it up, her eyes met Stephanie's. She broke into a wide grin and waved. She glanced at the crowded counter, then yelled to Stephanie over the noise. "I'll be over in a sec!"

Stephanie nodded and watched curiously as Brandi headed toward the counter. She stopped and leaned over a boy who sat on the last round swivel stool, near the jukebox. His back was to Stephanie. He wore a cap and his jacket collar was raised. All she could see was that he had dark hair.

*That's funny*, she thought. *Brandi doesn't know*

*anybody in San Francisco.* She shrugged. *Maybe it's a boy she met on the* Sunshine *today.*

Brandi gave the guy a big hug and kissed him on both cheeks. *They're really good friends if they just met today,* Stephanie thought in surprise.

Brandi whispered something to the boy, then hurried over to Stephanie's booth. Allie slid over to make room for her.

"Hi, guys," she greeted them. "How are you doing?"

"Great," Stephanie told her. "We were just talking about our float for the competition."

Brandi's dark eyes gleamed. She leaned her elbows on the table. "I've got a great idea for a float. Do you want to hear it?"

"Sure!" Stephanie leaned forward, too.

"I call it 'The Living Statue Garden,'" Brandi told them. "You fix the float to look like a garden, and you paint yourselves to look like statues."

"That's kind of wild," Allie said. "Do you need special paint for that?"

"Yeah. This kind." Brandi held out her wrist to show Allie and the others the watch painted on her skin.

"That is incredible!" Allie exclaimed.

"I never saw anything like it," Darcy added. "You are really talented, Brandi."

"That settles it. Living statues is a fantastic idea for our float," Stephanie said. "We've got to use it! But only if you agree to work with us," she added to Brandi.

"Deal!" Brandi seemed pleased.

*This is great,* Stephanie thought. *With Brandi's help, we'll build a truly awesome float. We'll slaughter those Flamingoes!*

"I'm going to play some music to celebrate." Stephanie grabbed a few quarters out of her bag and hurried to the jukebox.

She had to squeeze past the boy Brandi knew. "Zack and the Zees," she muttered as she scanned the list. She found their latest hit, then slid a quarter into the slot.

She turned around—and found herself staring at Brandi's friend. He stared back and Stephanie caught her breath. There was something awfully familiar about him. Those deep blue eyes . . . the dark brows . . . and the tiny scar near his right eye.

Stephanie inhaled deeply. Her legs nearly collapsed under her. Her heart did a wild flip-flop. For a moment she thought she was going to faint.

*Am I dreaming?* she wondered. *Or can it really be him? In person?!*

*Stay calm*, Stephanie told herself. *Take a close look, but stay calm!*

It *was* him!

Zack.

Zack of the Zees!

She couldn't believe it. Zack. Right here at the Galaxy Grill. Sitting right there . . . looking at her!

Zack's eyes darted to either side. He pulled his cap lower to hide more of his face and raised a finger to his lips.

"Please, don't give me away," he whispered. "I just sneaked in for some food. I didn't know this place would be so mobbed."

Stephanie nodded. Zack didn't want to be swarmed by people screaming and begging for his autograph. She stared as the waitress handed Zack a bag of takeout food. He slid off the stool and practically sneaked out of the diner.

Stephanie slowly turned around to find Brandi standing behind her. Stephanie grabbed her arm. "You know him," she whispered. "You actually know Zack!"

Brandi grinned. "You're not excited or anything, are you?" she teased.

"Are you guys dating?" Stephanie asked. "I saw you give him a hug."

Brandi crinkled up her nose. "No way! Why?" she asked. "Are you interested?"

Stephanie felt her mouth drop open. "Yes! Who wouldn't be?"

"I wouldn't," Brandi answered with a shrug. "Zack . . . well, I just don't find him, um, interesting in a dating kind of way."

"I think he's awesome," Stephanie declared.

Brandi smiled at her. "You know, we're having a barbecue on the yacht tomorrow afternoon. Zack will be there. Would you like to come along?"

"Are you kidding? Yes!" Stephanie grabbed the table to keep from floating up to the ceiling. She'd just entered total heaven!

Zack wasn't just a handsome face on a CD cover anymore. He was someone she'd actually met. Someone she'd kept a secret for. And tomorrow she was going to a party with him.

She was going to a party with her perfect guy!

# CHAPTER
# 5

◆ ◂ ◂ ◆

"Where is Brandi, anyway?" Stephanie scanned the deck of the *Sunshine*.

She and her friends and the rest of the crew were gathered at the bow for their sailing lessons. Ryan and Jenny taught the others while Josh was in charge of her group. He was just finishing explaining how to catch enough wind to sail when it was a very calm day. The big boat rocked gently on the water and the sun was warm.

It was a perfect day for a barbecue—but Brandi hadn't shown up at Summer Sail.

"What if she never comes?" Stephanie asked, worried. "Am I still invited to her party?"

"Of course," Darcy told her. "Brandi will show up before then."

"Yeah. Maybe she's just the type who's always late for things," Kayla said with a shrug.

"She missed the whole morning," Stephanie pointed out. "She missed chores, and sailing practice, and now our lesson."

"Maybe she had to stay at the yacht. To help get ready for the barbecue," Allie said in a low voice.

"Maybe." Stephanie glanced across the dock to where Brandi's sleek yacht was moored. "It doesn't look like anyone on board is awake yet," she said. "And it's almost time for the barbecue."

"Maybe music-business people sleep late," Kayla suggested.

Stephanie sighed. "I just hope they don't forget about their own barbecue," she said.

"You mean, you hope they don't forget to ask *Zack* over for their barbecue," Darcy teased.

"Right," Stephanie replied.

"Well, you look great, Steph," Allie told her.

"Do I? Thanks," Stephanie told her. She had worn one of her favorite outfits: dark purple corduroy shorts and a striped crop top. Her hair was pulled back in a long, braided ponytail with a matching purple scrunchie.

"I wanted to look good," Stephanie added. "But not so good that the Flamingoes would guess I have someplace special to go."

"This is the biggest secret we've ever kept from the Flamingoes," Allie said.

"And the best," Darcy added.

Kayla nodded in agreement. "I still think we should tell Darah about it," she said. "This is something to brag about."

"Darah would never *stop* bragging if she was invited to a party with Zack," Kayla pointed out.

Stephanie firmly shook her head. "Sorry. We are keeping this a total secret until the barbecue is over. If Darah finds out, she'll ruin it for me somehow. I know she will."

"Yeah—she'd probably invite *herself* over." Allie giggled.

"In a second," Stephanie agreed. "That's why we have to keep this a total secret from the Flamingoes."

"When the barbecue is over," Darcy said, "we can brag all we want."

"Right," Stephanie agreed. She glanced toward the Flamingoes to make sure they couldn't hear what Stephanie and her friends were saying.

She noticed that Darah looked especially nice that morning. She was wearing a great new pale pink and white skirt outfit with matching pink canvas platform sneakers. A short scarf was knotted around her neck.

*I hate to admit it, but she looks terrific*, Stephanie thought. *Only a Flamingo would get so dressed up for a regular day at Summer Sail.*

"You know, I'm a little nervous about seeing you-know-who today," Stephanie said.

"Why?" Kayla asked in surprise.

Stephanie lowered her voice to a whisper. "Well, it was really cool meeting Zack at the diner yesterday. I mean, he seemed like such a regular guy. But—" She swallowed hard.

"What will I say to him?" she blurted out. "What if I can't think of anything to say? What if he thinks I'm a total jerk?"

"I thought you said he was a regular guy," Allie replied in a sensible voice. "So you'll talk about regular stuff."

"Allie's right, Steph," Kayla assured her. "You have nothing to worry about. You're lots of fun to talk to."

Josh's voice interrupted their conversation. "Any questions, Stephanie?" he asked, looking right at her. "You usually have a lot to say in class."

Stephanie felt her cheeks turn red. She hadn't

37

heard a word Josh said for the last few minutes. He probably knew it, too.

"Uh, no questions," she murmured.

"Okay," Josh said. "Then before we call it a day, I'd like the float teams to meet for a minute. Just to make sure you all agree on your projects."

The crowd broke up and formed into teams. Stephanie noticed the Flamingoes giggling wildly over something.

As Stephanie watched, Mary passed Cynthia a sheet of paper. They noticed Stephanie looking. With a sly grin, Cynthia handed Stephanie the paper.

Stephanie stared at it wordlessly. It was a photograph of Zack that was clipped from a music magazine. Someone had made a Xerox copy of a photo of Darah and taped it next to Zack. It made it look as if Darah and Zack were on-stage together.

"In your dreams!" Stephanie exclaimed.

"Let me see that," Anna demanded. Stephanie showed it to her. Anna made a face, then showed the page to Allie, Darcy, and Kayla.

"Phony photographs are the closest you'll ever get to Zack," Kayla told Cynthia.

"Oh, really?" Cynthia sneered. "That shows

what *you* know!" She nudged Tiffany. Tiffany giggled.

"You'd probably be thrilled to be in a phony photo with Zack," Tiffany added.

"You'd be thrilled to read about him," Cynthia said.

Stephanie had to bite her lip to keep from saying anything.

Darah raised an eyebrow. "Well, some of us are going to do more than read about him," she said. "Because it just so happens that Brandi invited me to a barbecue on her yacht today. And guess who I'm going to meet? Zack!"

# CHAPTER
# 6

"You can't be going!" Stephanie exclaimed. "Brandi asked *me* to her barbecue."

Darah acted astonished. Then she quickly composed herself and tossed her head. "Well, I didn't know any losers would be there."

"Who are you calling a loser?" Stephanie's voice rose in anger.

"If the shoe fits . . ." Darah said with a coy smile.

"Look, Darah, I don't know how you got invited," Stephanie said. "But Brandi asked me because—"

"Steph!" Kayla interrupted. "Don't waste your breath." Allie nodded in agreement.

Tiffany grasped Darah's arm. "Who cares

about her?" Tiffany said. "Brandi probably felt sorry for her. That's why she invited her. Anyway, Zack would never pay attention to a loser like Stephanie."

"Not if you're there," Cynthia added.

"You're right. What was I thinking?" Darah linked arms with Tiffany and strolled down the gangplank. At the bottom she turned toward Brandi's yacht.

Stephanie watched her go with a sick feeling in the bottom of her stomach. "I can't believe it," she murmured. "I can't believe Brandi invited Darah, too."

"I *don't* believe it," Darcy declared. "I bet Darah is lying. I bet she made the whole thing up!"

"Could be," Allie said. "I wouldn't put it past her."

"Even Darah wouldn't do that," Stephanie said. "At the barbecue I'll be able to find out in a second if Darah was invited."

"I don't know why you're acting so surprised," Anna told her. "Why shouldn't Brandi invite Darah? She hung out with the Flamingoes yesterday."

"But—I'm the one who kept Zack's secret last night," Stephanie protested. "That's why Brandi invited me. Why would she invite Darah?"

"Who knows," Darcy said in a brisk tone. "But I do know one thing. You'd better get over to that barbecue—before Darah monopolizes Zack!"

Stephanie's heart pounded with excitement as she headed up the gangplank to Brandi's yacht. It was definitely set up for a party.

Long tables piled with platters of food and drinks lined the side of the boat that faced the harbor.

*That's why I didn't see signs of a party from the* Sunshine, Stephanie realized.

A small crowd was gathered around the gas-powered barbecues, talking and laughing. Stephanie glanced around, trying to catch sight of Brandi.

Stephanie crossed the deck. It almost seemed to glow in the sunlight. The brass rails were as shiny as mirrors.

"Hey, Stephanie!"

Stephanie whirled around to see Brandi hurrying toward her. She caught her breath. Walking behind Brandi was Zack.

For a second Stephanie thought she might faint. She had to take a deep breath to calm herself.

Zack looked even cuter today than he had last

night. He wore a black T-shirt, jeans, and a single silver earring.

Then she noticed Darah hurrying along behind him.

Zack wasn't paying much attention to Darah. He did grin when he saw Stephanie, though.

"Stephanie! I'm glad you came," Brandi announced. "Sorry I wasn't at sailing, but I felt sick earlier. Zack, this is Stephanie," she said.

"Oh, I already know her." Zack grinned. "She's the girl who saved me last night. Hey," he said.

"Hey," Stephanie answered, trying to sound casual.

"Saved you?" Darah butted in. She stared at Zack. "What do you mean by that? How did she save you?" She looked so upset that Stephanie almost laughed.

Zack gave Darah a serious look. "She recognized me at the diner," he explained. "But when I asked her not to say anything, she didn't. You have no idea what it's like to deal with fans sometimes. She saved me from a mob scene."

Darah flushed.

"I guess some fans do get carried away," Stephanie said.

"Yeah," Zack said. "But I like my fans. I mean,

they made our band a hit. It's just that sometimes, I need to be alone.''

"I can understand that.'' Stephanie smiled at
him so hard, it almost hurt her cheeks.

*Stop grinning at him like an idiot,* she told herself. *He'll think you're totally lame!*

Zack grinned back at her as if she'd said something special.

Then, for an awful moment, she couldn't think
of anything to say next.

*Talk,* she ordered herself. *Say something—anything—before Darah tries to take over!*

Luckily, Brandi rescued her. "Hey, Stephanie,''
she said, "want me to draw something on you?''
She held out her left arm. It was painted with a
sun, moon, and stars.

"You should let her,'' Zack said. "Brandi
paints the coolest fake tattoos I've ever seen.''

"That is an incredible one,'' Darah said, nod-
ding at Brandi's arm.

"I can paint one on you, too,'' Brandi offered.

"Sure!'' Darah's eyes lit up. Stephanie was
sure Darah would agree to get a real tattoo—if
Brandi suggested it. "I'll even go first.''

"Okay. Come with me.'' Brandi dragged
Darah toward the opposite end of the yacht.

Zack turned to Stephanie. "Do you know how
to play pool?'' he asked.

"Uh, just a little," she answered.

"That's okay. I'm a pretty good teacher. Let's try it." Zack led the way into one of the cabins. It was fixed up like a game room with a giant pool table in the middle.

He pulled two pool cues from the rack on the wall and rubbed the tips with chalk so the cue wouldn't slip off the ball. Then he racked the balls on the table.

"Know how to break?" he asked.

"Not really," Stephanie admitted.

Zack showed her how to hold the cue and where to aim to make the balls spread out across the table. Stephanie tried to do as he said. She held her breath and shot.

She watched in awe as the pool balls spun out. One striped ball dropped neatly into the corner pocket.

"Good shot. You're a natural," Zack exclaimed. "Now try to get that purple striped ball into the side pocket."

Stephanie shot. "I did it!" She stared at Zack in amazement.

"Tell me again you play only a little," Zack teased. "You're really a pro, right?"

"No," she replied, blushing a bit.

*This is unbelievable*, she told herself. Not only

45

was Zack totally cool, he was also totally nice. *I think I'm in love!*

She sank three more balls while Zack beamed at her in admiration.

"We're back!" Brandi called from the doorway. She and Darah hurried into the room. Darah held out her right arm to show off a long, curving green snake painted with bright red eyes. Brandi had painted it so it wrapped around her arm from her elbow down to her wrist.

"That is amazing," Stephanie said.

"I'll do yours now," Brandi offered.

"You know, I'm really hungry," Zack interrupted. "We should eat before the food is gone."

"You're right, Zack," Darah immediately answered. "I'm starving, too."

"Great. Then you won't mind bringing back a couple of burgers for Stephanie and me," Zack said. "We can't stop this game. Not until I get a chance to fight back. Stephanie is a killer pool shark!"

Darah's face turned dark red. "Well, I—" She sounded angry. Then she stopped and made an effort to sound pleasant. "I'd be glad to. I'll be right back." She stomped out of the room.

Stephanie could tell how angry Darah was. But she felt great!

*Zack did that so we could be alone,* she thought

46

in delight. *He likes me better than Darah. This must be the best day of my life!*

When Darah and Brandi came back with the food, they took turns eating and playing. They played for hours. Zack was shooting when Brandi turned to Stephanie and asked, "Want me to give you your tattoo now? The barbecue is almost over."

"Is it?" Stephanie glanced at her watch. Seven-thirty.

"Oh, no," she groaned. "I was supposed to be home half an hour ago! Sorry, Brandi, but I have to leave."

Darah's eyes lit up. "Really? It's too bad you have a curfew," she said.

Stephanie glared at Darah. "I don't have a curfew," she said. "But I promised to be home at seven, and I try to keep my promises." She reached for her backpack. "Thanks for inviting me," she told Brandi. "It's been great."

*The greatest afternoon of my life!* she thought.

Zack flashed her a smile. "See you," he said.

*I can't believe I have to go—and leave Darah with Zack!* Stephanie forced herself to say good-bye.

*By tomorrow, Darah will probably be bragging that she's Zack's girlfriend.* Stephanie left the cabin and started down the gangplank.

"Hey, Steph! Wait up," Zack called. He hurried to catch up to her. "Listen, I have a big meeting with Brandi's dad tomorrow. But would you have time to show me around San Francisco sometime?"

"Sure!" she burst out. "When?"

"How about the day after tomorrow?" Zack asked. "I'll pick you up early. We can spend the whole day together."

Somehow, she managed to answer in a normal-sounding voice. "Okay. Great." She added, "I'll see you then," after giving him her address.

She nearly skipped to the bike rack. She was so excited that she was surprised she didn't take off into the sky.

Zack wanted her to show him San Francisco!

*But not for two days*, she reminded herself. Two days seemed like a lifetime!

How would she live until then?

# CHAPTER

# 7

◆ ◀ ◆ ◆

"Where do you take a rock star?" Stephanie muttered.

She headed straight to the bookcases in the living room the second she got home. She searched the shelves for books about San Francisco and piled them on the coffee table. She flipped through them one by one.

There were tons of things to see and do in San Francisco—museums, parks, cable cars, Chinatown, and the Embarcadero section along the waterfront. The Golden Gate Bridge, and all of Golden Gate Park.

"First, I could take him on a cable car ride," she said, writing that down on her list.

Then she frowned. "But that will take only

about a half hour. And maybe he'll think a cable car ride is dumb."

With an irritated sigh, she scratched it out.

"We'll do the cable cars only on the way to something else," she decided. "But *what* something else?"

The front door banged open and D.J. flew into the house. "Hey, Steph!" her big sister called. "How's it going? Meet any new rock stars today?"

"Ha-ha," Stephanie answered, staring at the guide book.

D.J. strode into the living room and peered closely at Stephanie. "What's wrong? I thought you'd be on cloud nine. Didn't you have a great time today?"

"I had a super time, but now I'm in big trouble!" Stephanie wailed. "Zack asked me to show him San Francisco, and I don't know where to take him. I have to fill a whole day with great things to do—and I don't have a clue what they are!"

D.J. frowned. "That is a tough one," she admitted. She sat down next to Stephanie and glanced through a guidebook. "Didn't these give you any ideas?"

"They're full of ideas," Stephanie admitted. "But none of them are cool enough for a guy

50

like Zack. I want him to think I'm really sophisticated."

"Just be yourself, Steph," D.J. said. "You're fantastic the way you are."

"That is so lame, Deej," Stephanie replied. "That sounds like something Dad would say."

"Maybe Dad's right—for a change." D.J. laughed.

Stephanie frowned. "This is serious! Zack is used to doing super-cool stuff. What could I possibly show him that he's never seen before? What would impress him?"

D.J. sighed. "I gave you my best advice, Steph. Maybe you're making too much of this whole thing. If Zack likes you, he wants to spend time with you. Where you go isn't important."

"Right," Stephanie muttered.

D.J. shrugged. "I'm making it an early night. See you tomorrow." She bounded up the stairs to her room.

"Sure." Stephanie raked a hand through her hair. "Ohhhhhh!" she groaned. "I don't know what to do!"

She was still fretting when the rest of the family came home from a movie.

"Cousin Stephie!" Alex and Nicky, Aunt Becky and Uncle Jesse's five-year-old twins, made a mad dash for her.

"Hold it, you two!" Stephanie's aunt Becky grabbed the twins. "You'll get greasy popcorn fingers all over the furniture!"

"Up you go!" Her uncle Jesse scooped Alex up in one arm and Nicky in the other. "Your next stop is the bathtub," he told them.

"Mine, too," Joey Gladstone declared. Joey was Stephanie's dad's best friend. He had lived with the family for years, helping to take care of the kids. Joey was always funny and fun to be with. Sometimes, he acted more like a kid than a grown-up.

"I'm also covered with butter," Joey added. "I guess I have to have a bath also."

Stephanie shook her head in frustration. How could anyone in her family help her think of something to do for a sophisticated date? They were totally unsophisticated!

Stephanie's dad, Danny Tanner, crossed the living room. "Got to do a load of washing," he told Stephanie. "Do you have any more dirty clothes?" He stopped, noticing her glum expression.

"Honey? Is anything wrong?" he asked.

"Only everything!" Stephanie explained about her upcoming day with Zack. Danny put the dirty laundry down on the floor, picked up a guidebook from the coffee table, and thumbed through it.

"Steph, it's only a date," he said. "You've got to calm down about it. Just be yourself, honey."

Stephanie groaned. "That's exactly what D.J. said, and it doesn't help at all! This is a date with Zack—of Zack and the Zees. He's famous, Dad! How can I calm down?"

Danny shook his head. "Zack may be famous, but deep down inside he's a kid like any other kid."

Stephanie gave her father a look of total despair.

"Or maybe not," Danny added hastily. "Okay," he said. "Maybe a newspaper will help." He turned to the entertainment page. Stephanie peered over his shoulder while he checked out the listings.

"Wait—let me see that," she said. One headline was interesting. "Experience the work of some of the most outrageous young artists of our time," she read out loud. "Visit the new Lafayette Art Museum."

"Finally!" she exclaimed. "Something that's sophisticated—and different. This is definitely something Zack never saw before." She took the paper from her dad and scribbled down the address of the museum.

Then she noticed another listing. "Listen to this, Dad," she said. "There's a new café downtown called Grandpa's Left Foot. Doesn't the name sound cool? And it's not far from the museum." She wrote that address down, too.

"You see? I knew you'd work things out for yourself. Finish your list, and then get ready for bed," Danny told her. He smiled. "It's great to see you acting sure of yourself again," he added.

*Sure of myself?* Stephanie laughed. She didn't really feel sure of herself. She couldn't—not until her date with Zack was perfectly planned. Her perfect date!

# CHAPTER
# 8

◆ ◀ ◆ ◆

"Steph! Over here!" Allie waved her arms wildly as Stephanie turned into the marina parking lot early the next morning. Allie, Darcy, Kayla, and Anna had ridden on ahead and were already there.

"Hurry up," Kayla told her as Stephanie locked her bike into the rack. "We'll be late—and you know Josh hates it when we're late."

"Why did you guys wait for me, then?" Stephanie asked as she grabbed her backpack. They all hurried toward the *Sunshine*.

"We wanted to hear more about the barbecue," Allie told her.

"I told you everything last night," Stephanie said in surprise.

"Yeah, but we wanted to hear it all again," Kayla said. "Especially the part about Zack telling Darah to go get you food!"

Stephanie grinned. "That was pretty great," she agreed.

"But the best part is that Zack asked you out— and not Darah," Allie added.

"Yeah. Though I'm still worried about what happened after I left," Stephanie admitted. "What if Zack asked Darah out, too?"

"Or what if Darah asked *him* out," Kayla said.

"Didn't Brandi know what happened?" Allie asked.

"I don't know," Stephanie replied. "It was too late to call her."

"And you still don't know why she invited Darah to the barbecue?" Darcy asked.

"No. But we'll find out when Brandi gets here," Stephanie told her.

They hurried on board and the day began as Josh, Jenny, and Ryan handed out the morning assignments. Stephanie groaned when she found out she had deck duty. She wished she never had to scrub another foot of wooden planking again!

Brandi still wasn't there when chores were over and it was time for sailing practice. Darah and her group climbed into one of the larger, five-man sailboats. Stephanie and her friends squeezed into a smaller boat.

"We should have a large boat, too," Darcy muttered.

"We would," Kayla replied. "If our parents were rich and belonged to the yacht club."

Darah glanced their way. "Too bad you have a beginner boat," she called. "But then, they do assign them according to ability."

"If you knew what you were talking about, we might be insulted," Darcy snapped back.

Stephanie grinned. Darah simply turned her back.

They spent the next two hours practicing tacking—steering around the bright orange buoys in the harbor. Then they returned to the *Sunshine* for their usual group lesson.

Brandi still wasn't there.

"If Zack asked Darah on a date, we would have heard about it by now," Allie told Stephanie.

"I guess you're right," Stephanie replied.

"Just be glad that Darah's not giving you a hard time," Kayla added.

Josh taught an interesting lesson on foul-weather sailing. Finally he glanced at his watch. "I thought you'd all like to get started on your float projects today," he said.

"Finally!" Darcy whooped in excitement.

"Pull out the sketches of your ideas so I can check them," Josh went on. "I don't want any of you getting in over your heads."

Stephanie had totally forgotten that Josh asked them to bring along sketches. And Brandi hadn't mentioned it, either.

"Uh-oh," Stephanie said. "We don't have any sketches!"

"Yes, we do," Anna replied. She dug a sketch-book out of her backpack. "Of course, I'm not exactly sure what Brandi had in mind. But then, she wasn't here yesterday. So I couldn't ask her about it. I drew what I thought the living garden should look like."

"Wow. Thanks, Anna," Stephanie told her. "Though I guess we can't actually start working on our float until Brandi gets here."

"Why not?" Anna sounded annoyed. "We have the sketches."

"And what if she doesn't come at all today?" Darcy added.

"I'm sure she'll show up," Stephanie told her. "We have to wait for her."

Josh checked Anna's sketches and gave his approval. "Looks like we'll have a great flotilla," he said.

He reached into his pocket and pulled out a

handful of keys. "Here are your boathouse keys," he told the group. "You'll find boats and supplies waiting for you."

Josh called off the names of the teams. " . . . and Stephanie's group gets Boathouse Five. Darah, your team is in Boathouse Six."

"Six!" Darah gloated. "That's my lucky number! A lucky number for a winning team," she added, glancing at Stephanie.

Stephanie ignored her.

"Remember, people," Josh added. "You're responsible for keeping your boathouse tidy. And for locking up when you're not using it. So, what are you waiting for?" He grinned. "Let's get going!"

Stephanie, Darcy, Allie, Anna, and Kayla practically ran toward the northern end of the marina, where the boathouses were lined up along the waterfront. Each boathouse was about the size of a small garage.

They had white-painted wooden walls, tin roofs, and small windows to let in light and air. They sat half on the ground and half on stilts over the water. A set of double doors took up most of the front and back walls.

Stephanie unlocked the land-side doors and they walked in. A wide, wooden walkway, like a large dock, ran along the boathouse's three sides. Their small boat bobbed gently in the water.

"If we cover those windows with paper, we can keep our nosy neighbors from seeing what we're doing," Kayla pointed out.

"Good idea. And here are the supplies." Anna bent over a huge cardboard box filled with tissue paper, markers, paint, cardboard, wire, a staple gun, glue—even a hammer and nails.

"Well, if we can't wait for Brandi, let's just do simple things until she gets here," Stephanie instructed. "Anna, can you teach us how to make tissue-paper flowers?"

"Yes," Anna said.

"Good! Let's get started on the flowers, then," Stephanie replied. "We need a ton of them."

Anna, Darcy, Allie, and Kayla exchanged annoyed looks. Stephanie ignored them.

All the time they made paper flowers, Stephanie hoped that Brandi would show up. She didn't want to say it to Anna, but Brandi should be there to direct them. After all, the living garden was her idea.

An hour went by and still Brandi hadn't come. Stephanie glanced at the pile of paper flowers and sighed. "I just hope we're doing this right," she said.

"They look fine to me," Kayla replied.

"Don't worry," Anna said in a sarcastic voice. "I'm sure Stephanie would tell us if we were doing them wrong."

Stephanie glanced at her in surprise. "Why would I do that?" she asked.

Anna's eyes widened. "Because you've been acting like you're the boss of this whole project, that's why. Why do you think you are in charge?"

Stephanie felt her mouth drop open. "Who? Me?"

"Yes, you," Anna accused. "You wanted Brandi to be on our flotilla team, but you didn't bother to ask the rest of us how we felt."

"Yes, I did! Didn't I?" Stephanie thought hard. "We all agreed, at the diner."

"No, *you* decided," Anna declared. "And then you decided that we'd use her idea, too. After the rest of us had already agreed to use my whale idea."

"Hey, wait a minute—" Stephanie began.

"Hold on," Allie said. "Steph, Anna has a point. We did like Anna's whale idea. I mean, we also thought Brandi's idea was interesting, but you didn't really ask us which we liked best."

"It's not like we had to have a formal vote or anything," Stephanie protested.

"Why not?" Anna demanded. "We're going to put a lot of time and effort into this float. Why not vote on it?"

Stephanie glanced at her friends in disbelief. "You're not really mad, are you?"

"Not mad, exactly," Darcy told her. "But you did sort of take over. I mean, I understand that you were excited—and Brandi's idea is good." She shot an apologetic look at Anna. "But you still should have asked us," she ended.

"She's right," Kayla said. Allie nodded in agreement.

Stephanie felt horrible. "I didn't mean to be a tyrant," she told them. "But I like Brandi, and—"

"That's not the point," Anna declared. "You're acting totally starstruck. You're as bad as Darah! It seems like all you care about is impressing Brandi so you can hang out with her and her rock star friends."

"That's not fair," Stephanie protested. "You're not giving Brandi a chance. She's really sweet. And talented."

"If she's so great, why did she invite Darah to her barbecue?" Anna asked.

Stephanie felt a burst of impatience. "I don't know. But Brandi doesn't really know Darah or the Flamingoes. I guess she's just trying to make friends."

"Fine," Anna snapped. "Just don't act like she's some sort of goddess. I think there's something suspicious about her. I don't trust her."

"You're just mad because I like Brandi's float idea better than yours!" Stephanie exclaimed. "You're jealous."

"I am not!" Anna protested. "But I don't like the way you're acting."

"I don't like the way *you're* acting," Stephanie shot back. "You should be thrilled that I got to meet a great guy like Zack. Unless you're jealous about him, too!"

"That is s-so unfair!" Anna sputtered. "You're the one who can't stop talking about Mr. Perfect. I couldn't care less about throwing myself at some boy I don't even know."

"Guys, calm down," Darcy cut in. "This is getting really out of hand."

"I can't help it," Stephanie said. "She has no right to talk about Zack or Brandi that way!"

"If you think Brandi is so great, why isn't she here?" Anna demanded. "Her yacht is about fifty feet away. The truth is, she doesn't care about us or our float!"

"Maybe she'll be here tomorrow," Allie said,

trying to make peace. "You can call her tonight to find out, right, Steph?"

Stephanie gulped. "Uh, actually, I won't be here tomorrow." She felt a pang of guilt. "I've promised to show Zack around, remember? He's counting on us spending the whole day together."

"This is too much!" Anna fumed. "Now you're going to disappear on us, too?"

"Be fair," Stephanie protested. "This is *Zack* we're talking about."

"Oh, that's just great," Anna snapped. "Brandi doesn't bother to show up. And now you're going to leave all the work to us—while you're off having fun. You'd better decide what's more important. Our float—or your date with Zack."

Stephanie felt hurt and angry and confused all at the same time. Anna was completely wrong— about her, about Brandi, and most of all, about Zack.

Meeting him was one of the most important things that had ever happened to her. Why couldn't Anna see that?

"I'm sorry," Stephanie finally said. "But I won't be here tomorrow. I'll help twice as much the day after, but I won't miss the most important date of my life. And if you were really my friends, you wouldn't ask me to!"

# CHAPTER
# 9

◆ ◀ ✦ ◆

BUZZZZZZZZZZ!

For a second Stephanie thought she was dreaming about bees. She rolled over and tried to dream about something else.

BUZZZZZZZZZZ!

She sat up with a jolt. It wasn't bees, it was her alarm. Today was her date with Zack!

She reached over, hit the Off button, jumped out of bed, and headed for the bathroom.

She flicked the light on and peered at herself in the mirror. Her eyes were puffy. And . . . she gasped as she leaned toward her reflection.

Was that a pimple on her nose?

"Nooooooo!" she wailed. "It can't be."

But it was. No matter which way she turned,

she couldn't make it look like anything else. A big, fat pimple right on her nose! What a nightmare.

"You can do this," she said. "You can do this."

She jumped in the shower. When she was done, she searched for her emergency makeup. She managed to cover the pimple.

At least it didn't look like a stoplight on her face anymore. Her hair looked good. That was something.

She raced back to her room and pulled her favorite sundress out of her closet. She slipped it on and examined herself in the mirror.

*Perfect*, she thought. *Except for my nose!*

She would just have to be so full of personality that Zack wouldn't notice her nose, she decided. After lacing up her white sneakers, she was ready. As ready as she could ever be.

She raced downstairs and gulped down a breakfast drink. Danny entered the kitchen, tying his robe around him.

"Steph! Is that all you're going to eat?" he asked. "A healthy breakfast is an important part of—"

The loud roar of an engine interrupted his speech. He and Stephanie both hurried to the window as Zack pulled into the driveway on a big black motorcycle.

*A motorcycle!* Stephanie felt a wave of total dread. *Oh, no!*

No way would her dad let her go anywhere on a motorcycle!

*What will I tell Zack?* she worried. She could just imagine the scene her father would make:

*My daughter isn't allowed to ride a thing like that,* she heard Danny saying. *She's my little baby girl!*

Stephanie cringed. This was the worst thing that had ever happened to her! What was she going to do?

She snatched her shoulder bag and ran for the door. "See you, Dad!" she yelled.

"Hold on!" Danny followed her. Stephanie groaned. She should have known she couldn't escape that easily.

Her father followed her out to the driveway. He eyed Zack's motorcycle with distrust.

"Hi," Zack said, pulling his helmet off. "You must be Mr. Tanner. I'm Zack. Nice to meet you."

"Nice to meet you, too," Danny said. "Zack *what*, may I ask?"

Zack grinned. "Just Zack. I don't use my last name anymore."

"Uh-huh." Danny studied Zack's bike some more. He turned to Stephanie.

*Here it comes,* she thought. *He's going to forbid*

*me to go. He's going to totally humiliate me in front of Zack!*

But Zack spoke to her before her dad could say a word.

"Listen, Steph, I'm sorry," he said. "But I have only one helmet. You can't ride without one. We'll have to leave the bike here. Is that okay with you, Mr. Tanner?"

Her father's face lit up with a smile of relief. "That's just fine," he said.

Stephanie couldn't believe it. *I'm saved!* she thought. It must be a sign—her date *was* going to be a success, after all!

"Is there a bus or something we could take?" Zack asked.

"A bus?" Stephanie echoed. A date with a rock star—on a bus?

"Sure," Zack replied. "Why not?"

*Why not?* Stephanie thought. She'd still be with Zack.

"Okay. I'm game if you are," she said. She nodded good-bye to her dad as they hurried away.

"What are we doing first?" Zack asked as they walked to the nearby bus stop.

"There's a new museum I thought we could check out," Stephanie told him. "They're showing the most outrageous new artists. Does that sound all right?"

"Whatever you want to do is okay with me," Zack said.

They climbed onto the bus for the short ride to the museum. Stephanie was waiting for somebody to recognize Zack and make a fuss over him, but nobody did.

Probably no one would believe that the famous Zack would ride on a *bus!*

"I'm sorry we couldn't take your motorcycle," she told him.

"Hey, it's cool," Zack said. "I should have known better than to bring the bike. A lot of people don't want their kids riding them."

He smiled at her and placed a hand over one of hers. Stephanie felt a jolt of electricity run through her. Her heart bounced crazily.

*This must be a dream*, she thought. No way could she be sitting there, holding hands with Zack!

But it was real.

Zack held her hand until they reached their stop and climbed off the bus.

"This is it." Stephanie stared at the museum. It was four stories high, made of bright yellow stucco. Odd-shaped windows dotted the front and sides of the building. A flowering vine had been painted from the bottom of the building up to the roof.

"This is a wild-looking place," Zack remarked.

"It looks like something Brandi would paint," Stephanie replied.

Zack laughed. "You're right."

"Come on, let's go in," Stephanie said.

She had expected to find paintings inside, but the museum was filled with crazy sculptures. They all had motors and moved and twisted. Some looked as though they were trying to turn themselves inside out. One seemed to be trying to claw its way through the wall.

The sound system blasted bizarre recorded sounds—screeches and whistles.

"This *is* wild!" Stephanie was really enjoying herself as they strolled from room to room. She had never seen anything like it before.

"Which sculpture do you like best?" she asked Zack.

"That crawling one, I guess," he said. "What about you?"

"I kind of like—" she began.

Screeeeeeeechhhhh!

Stephanie saw Zack wince. She suddenly realized he didn't look as though he was having a very good time.

"Should we get out of here?" she asked.

"That is an incredibly good idea," Zack instantly agreed. He hurried to the exit. Stephanie stared after him in surprise.

*I didn't think he hated it that much,* she thought. She should have known this exhibit was too silly for a guy like Zack! She felt really dumb.

Zack was waiting for her on the front steps. "I have to admit I didn't get that stuff," he said.

"Well, I thought some of it was kind of interesting," Stephanie replied. "But then, I never saw anything like it before." *And you've probably been to museums like this a dozen times!*

Zack shrugged. "I guess they were trying to get a reaction out of us."

"Well, they did," Stephanie joked. "Yours was 'run'!"

Zack laughed so much that Stephanie began to feel better.

Except for the next big question: Where to go now? She'd planned to take Zack to lunch at Grandpa's Left Foot. But it was barely ten-thirty.

"Let's walk around for a while, okay?" she suggested, thinking fast. "This neighborhood is famous for its architecture—old Victorian houses that are painted in fantastic colors. They're called Painted Ladies."

"Sure," Zack agreed.

They turned down a street lined with the famous houses.

"Look at that one." Stephanie pointed to a house decorated with fancy, complicated carved wooden trim. "It looks like the witch's house in 'Hansel and Gretel,' doesn't it?"

"Uh-huh," Zack replied.

Stephanie waited for him to say more, but he made no other comment.

*Oops,* she thought. *Another mistake. I guess Zack doesn't care about architecture, either. He's probably seen lots more exciting buildings than these.*

She sighed. If only she could think of something—anything—that might really interest him.

They reached the edge of Golden Gate Park. "Um, there's lots of interesting stuff in the park," Stephanie said. She was beginning to feel desperate. "There's an amazing glass greenhouse—the Conservatory. And there's a Japanese teahouse with a real Japanese garden. Or we could take a hiking path. Or rent bicycles, or . . ." she trailed off. Everything she suggested sounded totally lame.

"Why don't we just hang out for a while?" Zack stretched out on the grass. "My meeting lasted all night yesterday. I'm beat."

"Sure," Stephanie said. She had bored him so totally, he had to lie down to recover!

She sat hugging her knees, trying not to stare at him.

*He really looks good in the sun,* she thought. *No, he would look good anywhere,* she corrected herself.

She tried to think of something to say. Magazine articles about dating always suggested asking the boy about himself.

"Uh, you travel a lot with the band now, don't you?" she asked.

"Yeah. We were on the road every day the last six months," he replied.

She leaned her chin on her knees. "Do you ever get tired of it?"

"Sure," he replied. "But it's the life, you know?"

Stephanie waited for him to say something more, but he closed his eyes and looked as if he wanted to go to sleep.

She felt another pang of disappointment. She was dying to learn more about him. But no way was she going to make a pest of herself.

She let her mind drift, imagining how great it would be if anyone she knew saw her with Zack of Zack and the Zees.

Why hadn't she planned it? She should have called everyone to tell them where they would be today!

*Except the Flamingoes,* she silently added. She

wouldn't want *them* to know where she was going with Zack. Just in case Darah showed up on their date!

The time crawled by. It was a pretty boring way to spend the morning. She glanced at her watch. Eleven-thirty. At least it was late enough to get lunch.

She leaned over and tapped Zack's shoulder. "It's nearly lunchtime," she said. "Maybe we should go."

Zack sat up. "Great. I'm starved."

They walked over to Grandpa's Left Foot.

*Please, please, please,* she thought as they pushed open the front door. *Let this be a really cool place!*

Inside, cigarette smoke filled the air. Stephanie coughed. She would have suggested they leave, but Zack didn't seem to mind. And then the hostess walked up to them.

"Table for two?" she asked. "Right this way." She led them to a corner and set menus on their table. "Is there anything I can do for you while you decide?"

"Yes," Stephanie said. "You can tell me why this place is called Grandpa's Left Foot."

"So that people will come in and ask," the hostess replied.

Zack laughed again. "Stephanie, you are so

funny," he said. Stephanie smiled. They ordered two Grandpa Specials and sat back, gazing out the windows through the cigarette smoke.

Zack started coughing. He took a long drink of water.

"Oh, no!" Stephanie exclaimed. "Is this smoke bad for your voice?"

"It's fine. Really," Zack insisted.

"Well . . . " Stephanie suddenly couldn't think of anything interesting to say.

She was terrified. She must be boring Zack out of his mind! Luckily, their food came.

*At least the sandwiches look interesting,* Stephanie thought. She and Zack both took giant bites.

"Delicious!" Stephanie exclaimed.

"Whoa! Hot!" Zack's eyes started to water. He gulped down his water. "I'm not crazy about spicy food."

"I'm so sorry," Stephanie cried. "We can order something else."

"That's okay. I'm not so hungry after all," Zack said. But she noticed that he ate every one of his french fries and finished the basket of bread on the table.

By then Stephanie could barely eat. Her stomach was twisted into knots. Zack was trying so hard to be nice to her. But their date was turning into a total disaster!

Things didn't get any better after lunch. Zack seemed bored by the Embarcadero, bored by the view of San Francisco's famous twisting, hilly streets from the top of Coit Tower, and even more bored on the cable car ride down to Fisherman's Wharf.

They finally ended the day at a special movie house where they showed new movies from Europe. Stephanie hoped the film would be sophisticated enough to interest Zack. But when she glanced his way, she saw that he had fallen asleep again.

*Great,* she groaned. *I put my date to sleep. Twice!*

When the movie ended, it was time to go home. Stephanie was miserable. She hadn't planned a single thing that interested Zack.

They walked to the bus stop in silence and rode to her street in silence. They walked to her house in silence.

It was horrible! Stephanie wished he would say something—anything! Obviously, he hated their date. He hadn't enjoyed one single thing.

She had never felt so awful in her life.

"Well, here we are!" She tried to sound cheerful as they reached her driveway.

"Yeah," Zack said.

She waited, feeling stupid and terrible as Zack

fastened his helmet and swung onto his motor-cycle. He gunned the engine.

"Well, bye, Steph," he called over the noise. "Thanks for the great day."

He zoomed off down the street. With a sinking heart Stephanie watched him go. She dragged herself into the house.

"Steph!" her dad called from the couch. "You're back! How did it go?"

She had to fight back tears to choke the words out, "Oh, Dad! I wanted today to be perfect. And it was. A perfect disaster!"

# CHAPTER
# 10

◆ ◀ ▪ ◆

The door to Stephanie's bedroom flew open. Stephanie sat up, rubbing her eyes. She was trying to sleep late. Michelle had already left for day camp, and she was enjoying the peace and quiet.

Besides, she couldn't face the day. She couldn't face anyone.

"What's going on?" Allie cried as she and Darcy burst into Stephanie's room. They flung themselves onto the foot of her bed.

"Tell us everything!" Darcy demanded.

"I guess you got home too late to call us last night, right?" Allie asked. "Was it wonderful?"

Stephanie bit her lip. "It was awful," she admitted. "I totally blew it with Zack." She told them everything about the day and how she had bored Zack completely.

"I can't face going to the marina," she finished. "What if Zack is there visiting Brandi and he sees me? He'll probably pretend he doesn't know me!"

Allie and Darcy exchanged uncertain glances. "You probably just *think* Zack was bored," Allie said, forcing a smile. "You were nervous and all."

"Right," Darcy agreed. "It couldn't have been as bad as you think."

"Believe me, it was." Stephanie swung her legs over the side of her bed. "I should stay home and hide for the rest of my life."

"You can't do that," Allie told her. "Listen, Josh gave us the day off from lessons and sailing. We can work on the float all day. You should see how great it's coming along."

"It is?" Stephanie asked.

"Yeah. Brandi showed up yesterday," Darcy explained. "She spent a lot of time working with us. She had some pretty good ideas. Even Anna liked them."

"She did?" Stephanie felt a little better. "Then I guess Anna isn't suspicious of Brandi anymore."

"Well, maybe a little," Darcy replied.

Allie opened Stephanie's bureau drawers and pulled out a pair of jean shorts and a yellow crop top. "Here," she said, tossing them to Stephanie. "Get dressed."

"But are you guys still mad at Brandi?" Stephanie asked as she pulled on her clothes.

Allie shook her head. "We all feel better now that the float is shaping up so well."

Stephanie fastened her gold ankle bracelet and pulled on sneakers. She grabbed a muffin. Then she, Allie, and Darcy hurried to the marina. Stephanie instantly checked out Brandi's yacht.

No sign of Zack.

That was a relief. They crossed the lawn to Boathouse Five. Darcy knocked and Kayla opened the door. "Hi, guys," she said. "We were getting worried about you."

"I overslept because—" Stephanie started to explain. Her mouth dropped open. The float looked incredible! "You guys!" she exclaimed. "You must have worked like crazy yesterday."

They had made cutouts for tree trunks and stapled on hundreds of fringed palm leaves. They almost looked real.

"We plan to drape the flowers around the tree trunks today," Kayla said. "Then we're going to fill the entire float with more flowers."

Stephanie shook her head in admiration. "It's awesome!"

"Isn't it?"

Brandi stepped through the door.

"Brandi!" Stephanie was glad to see her—and then nervous. Zack had probably told her every detail of their awful date. Now Brandi must think she was a total loser.

"Hi, Steph! I feel like we haven't talked for days," Brandi said. "Yesterday—" she started.

*Here it comes!* Stephanie winced. *Here's where she tells me what a jerk Zack thinks I am!*

Brandi beamed at her. "Zack told me he had a great time yesterday. A really great time! What did you do to him, anyway? He thinks you're so funny and interesting."

Stephanie's mouth dropped open. "Really?" She couldn't believe her ears.

"Totally. You really impressed him," Brandi said. "I think he's dying to ask you out again."

Stephanie could only stare at her in astonishment. "But . . . I thought, that he thought . . ."

*Zack likes me!* She felt a burst of excitement. *Zack likes me!*

"See? You worried for nothing. This is great," Darcy told her.

"Yeah," Allie added. "Now you can stop worrying about whether he likes you or not—and get back to work on our float."

"That will be a relief," Anna said.

Stephanie shot her a look. Anna still wasn't giving her much credit for caring about the float, she realized.

"No problem." Stephanie felt wonderful now. "I can't wait to help out."

"Wait a minute." Brandi looked uncomfortable. "I was thinking. Actually, there's something I need to tell you about the float . . ." She hesitated.

"What? What's wrong with it?" Anna demanded. "You liked it well enough yesterday."

"I know, I know," Brandi told her. "You guys did an incredible job. I . . . I just had some ideas about changing it."

"Why?" they all blurted out at once.

Anna raised her eyebrows. "I think we even improved on your idea."

"You did!" Brandi exclaimed. "But, I thought, maybe we could make it even better. More original. Like, we could turn the trees into fancy pillars, or—"

"No way," Anna said. "It looks fantastic. And it's almost done."

"She's right, Brandi." Darcy exchanged glances with Anna. Stephanie realized that Darcy was acting annoyed now, too. So were Allie and Kayla.

"We're not changing anything," Darcy added.

"Okay. I just thought I'd ask. I don't want to make anybody upset," Brandi said. "Uh—I have something to do right now, though. I'll be back later. Okay?"

Brandi dashed out of the boathouse before anyone could answer. Stephanie stared after her in surprise. "That was weird."

"Did we insult her or something?" Kayla asked.

"I don't think so," Allie replied. "She left early yesterday, too, remember?"

"But she didn't even stay ten minutes today!" Anna exclaimed. She turned to Stephanie. "She's your friend. Why is she acting so weird?"

"I don't have a clue," Stephanie answered.

"Of course not," Darcy teased. "You're probably too busy dreaming about your next date with Zack. Maybe he'll bring the Zees along to give you a private concert."

Stephanie blushed as her friends all began teasing her. *At least they're not complaining about Brandi anymore,* she thought.

They spent the next few hours working on the float. Stephanie was sure that if she folded one more tissue-paper flower, she'd have nightmares about them.

But she felt guilty about missing work the day before, so she didn't complain.

Besides, she felt great. *Zack likes me. Zack likes me* ran through her mind like a song.

They worked hard until it was time to go home.

"Whew!" Darcy breathed. "That was a long day."

"Do you guys want to stop at the Galaxy Grill on the way home?" Stephanie asked. She wasn't afraid of bumping into Zack anymore. In fact, she couldn't wait to see him. Maybe he would be at the diner, and he would ask her out again.

"I'm dying for a strawberry shake," Allie said.

They locked up and stepped outside. Darah's high-pitched laugh echoed through the air. Stephanie shaded her eyes and peered at the Flamingoes' boathouse.

Darah, Tiffany, and the others were also locking up for the day.

Brandi was with them—talking and laughing as if they were best friends.

"I don't believe it!" Darcy exclaimed. "She left us to spend the day with the Flamingoes."

"I told you I didn't trust her," Anna said.

Stephanie felt confused as she watched Brandi

walk off with Darah. "But it doesn't mean anything," she reminded her friends. "We know that she is friends with Darah."

"What was she doing with them all day?" Anna asked.

"And why didn't she come back to help us, like she said?" Darcy added. Allie and Kayla exchanged a glance. They all turned to look at Stephanie.

"I'm sure there's a good explanation," she said.

Anna looked doubtful. "I want to see what they were doing in there," she declared.

Anna stormed up to the Flamingoes' boathouse and peered through the crack between the doors. When she turned around, there was a strange expression on her face.

"Oh, there's a good explanation, all right," she said. "Come look at this!"

Stephanie had a feeling of dread as she approached the doors. She stepped close to Anna and peered through the crack. She could just make out the Flamingoes' float in the dim light.

It was a living garden.

# CHAPTER

# 11

◆  ◀  ✦  ◆

Stephanie felt as though somebody had punched her in the stomach. Anna was right all along.

Brandi wasn't a friend. She was a traitor. A spy!

And she had given the Flamingoes the same idea for a float!

Allie, Darcy, and Kayla crowded around Stephanie, straining to get a look in the boathouse. Stephanie expected them to start shouting in anger. Instead, there was an eerie silence.

Stephanie didn't know what to say. The worst thing was, she felt as if it were all her fault. She was the one who trusted Brandi. She was the one who insisted Brandi be on their team.

Then she heard Brandi's voice calling in the

distance. "Oh, no! I forgot my backpack," Brandi said. "Darah—toss me the boathouse key. I'll get it and catch up with you later!"

Stephanie and the others stood frozen in silence as Brandi ran toward the Flamingoes' boathouse. She stopped in her tracks the moment she saw them.

Stephanie could barely look her in the face. Darcy, Allie, Anna, and Kayla glared at her.

Brandi looked from one to the other. "I can explain," she began. "It's not what you think!"

"Oh, no?" Stephanie turned and began to walk away.

"Stephanie!" Brandi yelled after her. "Please! I can explain everything! Really!"

Stephanie walked faster. She couldn't bear to hear any phony excuses. Her friends hurried alongside her.

Nobody said a word until they had jumped on their bikes and pedaled well away from the marina.

"What was she thinking?" Stephanie finally exploded. "Why did she give the Flamingoes our idea?"

"It wasn't our idea," Anna said in a quiet voice. "It was Brandi's. You're the one who made it into our idea."

Stephanie bit her lip. Anna was right. But she didn't have to rub it in.

She sighed. "Okay, Anna, I guess I deserved that," she said. "You were right about Brandi all along. I apologize for not listening to you. I apologize for everything."

"That's all right," Anna said. "I was mad. But I guess you just got carried away. I mean, Brandi did introduce you to your rock-star boyfriend."

"He's not my boyfriend," Stephanie protested. "And I can't even think about Zack right now. All I can think of is how Brandi let me down. Let all of us down."

"How we did all that work for nothing!" Darcy shook her head in disgust.

"What should we do?" Allie asked.

"I don't know yet," Stephanie told her. "Let's all go home and think about it. We'll talk later."

They all agreed. Stephanie headed home and ate a dinner she barely tasted. She knew she should be coming up with a brilliant idea for another float. But all she could think about was what a traitor Brandi was. As soon as she finished eating she ran up to her room and threw herself on her bed.

*Brandi was a traitor*, she thought over and over again. She knew it was true. How could she have ever trusted her? How could she have been so dumb?

*I really liked her,* she thought. No. She liked the person Brandi had seemed to be. Not the person she really was.

Maybe she could figure out what to do about the float. Not that she could make any decisions without talking to the others. At least she'd learned her lesson about that!

"Steph?" D.J. knocked on the door and poked her head into the room. "Zack called this afternoon."

Stephanie sat bolt upright. "Zack!"

"He said he'd call back later." D.J. grinned. "My little sister, going out with a rock star! Maybe I should ask you to fix me up with one of his friends," she teased.

Stephanie ignored her. "When later?" she asked.

"He didn't say," D.J. replied.

Stephanie groaned. "Thanks anyway, Deej." If she hadn't been so upset about Brandi, she would have jumped up and started dancing around the room. Zack had really called!

*Wait a minute,* she thought. *That means Brandi was telling the truth about our date.*

Why would she tell the truth about Zack but lie about the Flamingoes? It didn't make sense.

Rinnnnnnnng!

Stephanie ran into her dad's study and dove for the phone. She made herself take a deep breath before she answered. "Hello?"

"Stephanie? This is Josh."

Her heart sank. "Oh. Hi, Josh. What's up?"

"I was worried about you," he said. "You never missed a day of Summer Sail before yesterday. Are you okay?"

"Oh. Sure, I'm fine," Stephanie told him.

"Good. Then everything is okay with your float team?" he asked.

Stephanie hesitated. Should she tell him about the mixup with Brandi? Maybe she could ask him to give them extra time to build their float.

*He can't change the date of the whole flotilla for you*, she realized.

"Um, things are okay, for now," she said. "Maybe we should talk more tomorrow."

"All right," Josh told her. "How about after the sailing lesson? I'll have some time then."

"That would be great," Stephanie said. She had just hung up, when the phone rang again. *It's probably Josh calling back. He's probably wondering why I sounded so strange*, she thought. She lifted the receiver.

"Josh?" she said.

"Stephanie? It's Zack."

*Oops!* She nearly dropped the phone. "Zack—hi! I, uh, was just talking to my sailing instructor. His name is Josh. I thought you were him. I mean—" She paused. *Why am I babbling to him about Josh?* She could kick herself for acting so dumb.

"Listen, I have some free time tonight. Want to go out again?" he asked.

"Tonight? Sure. I think it will be okay," she said.

"Great. I'll pick you up in a half hour," he said.

They hung up. This time Stephanie really did jump up and down.

She had another chance with Zack!

*And this time,* she told herself, *I am going to get things right!*

# CHAPTER

# 12

◆ ◂ ◂ ◆

The roar of Zack's motorcycle echoed in the driveway.

"He's here!" Stephanie raced to the front door. She had changed into a flowered skirt and yellow T-shirt under a black denim vest.

A few minutes later Zack rang the front bell. Stephanie took a deep breath, then opened it. Zack looked as cute as ever.

"Hi!" he greeted her. "We have a great plan. I found out that we can take a sunset boat ride. Is that okay with you, Steph? I already reserved one of the marina's little rowboats. We can't leave the harbor, of course, but I hear the sunsets are awesome."

Stephanie's eyes sparkled. "That sounds perfect!"

She called good-bye to her family, grabbed her shoulder bag, and they were on their way. "How about taking a cable car partway there?" she asked.

"Sure," Zack answered. "That would be okay. Do you ride a cable car to school?"

"Oh, no," she told him, glad that he'd started a conversation. "They don't go anywhere near my school."

"I like that they run on electricity," Zack said. "No pollution," he added. "But the only thing I can't figure out is how they stop them."

Stephanie stared at him in confusion. Was he teasing her? "They use the brakes," she said.

"Oh, yeah, right!" He snapped his fingers. "Maybe I could use a cable car in a music video."

Stephanie tried not to wonder why he'd asked such a silly question. "Using a cable car in a video would be great," she said. "Are you making one soon?"

"Oh, no," Zack said. "Not for a while. Not until our next CD comes out."

"Oh. Well, when is your next CD coming out?" she asked.

"In August, I think." Zack headed up the

block toward the bus stop. Stephanie walked alongside him.

This date was already going better than their last one. At least, Zack was talking more.

*I guess I'll stick to talking about music for a while,* she thought. That wouldn't bore him.

"So, did you use all new material on that CD?" she asked. "Did you write new songs for it?"

"Oh, I don't write the songs," Zack said. "That's really, really hard. I just sing them."

"Right. It's hard." Stephanie felt a stab of disappointment. *Well, not everyone is a songwriter,* she told herself.

They caught the bus and rode to the nearest cable car stop.

*Stick to music,* Stephanie reminded herself as they waited.

"So, what can we expect next from the Zees?" she asked. "You're not becoming a country band or anything, are you?"

"No," he said, laughing. "That's a good one, Steph. No, we're still the Zees, don't worry."

"Uh-huh." She smiled, waiting for him to go on. But he was silent again.

The cable car arrived. Zack took her hand when they found seats inside. Stephanie waited to feel the jolt of electricity—but nothing happened this time.

Stephanie frowned. The evening started off so well. But now . . .

She kept trying to start another conversation, but it was tough going. Zack barely replied to anything she said. And he thought even her simplest comments were hilarious.

If it was anyone else, she would have thought him kind of . . . boring.

But he was Zack. A famous musician!

It had to be her fault. Maybe she was asking the wrong questions again.

They reached the marina and headed down to the dock. Stephanie loved the way the water reflected in the fading light. They picked up their boat and Zack hopped in and held out a hand to help her.

"Do you know how to row?" he asked as she sat down. "Because I don't."

"Oh." Stephanie shot him a questioning look. "It's not very hard. I could show you how to do it."

"Nah. I'm kind of tired," Zack said.

*Then why did you ask me to go rowing?* Stephanie wondered. She almost felt annoyed. But how could she be annoyed with Zack?

He leaned back as she rowed. The bay was as

smooth as satin, and it was so quiet that the only sound was the gentle splash of her oars in the water.

"This will be beautiful when the sun sets," she said.

"I guess so," he answered.

"You guess so?" Stephanie grinned. "I thought you said the sunsets are awesome. Isn't that why you wanted to come?"

"Well, one of the guys in the band said the sunsets are awesome," Zack replied. "I never noticed them much. But he suggested I bring you here. I wasn't sure what to do tonight. It's hard to think of fun stuff."

"Yeah, it is," Stephanie agreed. She wasn't sure what else to say. She tried not to feel disappointed again. After all, it didn't really matter whose idea the sunset ride was. And she didn't expect Zack to quote poetry about it or anything.

*But a little enthusiasm would be nice*, she couldn't help thinking.

She found herself stifling a yawn. Zack noticed and grinned.

"You're tired, too," he said. "You know, I don't sleep that well in hotels."

He launched into a long speech about all the different hotels he had stayed in. Mostly, he talked about room service.

It was the most he had ever talked. Stephanie never dreamed anyone could talk about hamburgers in such detail.

She stretched her arms. They were beginning to ache. She began to think longingly of her bed. This date was as bad as the first one.

*I want to go home*, she thought. *I'm so bored I could scream!*

She stopped rowing as an amazing thought struck her. She wasn't to blame for their awful dates. Zack was!

She really hadn't bored him. He thought she was terrific. She was the one who was bored. Zack was . . . well, dull.

With a sigh, she turned the boat and headed into the marina. Zack sat forward, surprise on his face.

"We're going back already?" he asked.

"We're not allowed to be out here after dark," she told him.

"Oh. What about the awesome sunset?" Zack asked

"You missed it," Stephanie told him. "I think you were talking about the hamburgers in your Chicago hotel."

Zack laughed as if she had said something really funny again. "You know what, Steph?" he asked. "I never met anyone who was so much

97

fun to talk to. We've had some great conversations.''

Stephanie almost laughed, but she didn't want to hurt his feelings. He was a nice guy. He just didn't know that a conversation took more than one person talking!

Back at the dock, Stephanie tied the boat securely. Zack hopped out and grasped her hand as he helped her climb out. This time she didn't even try to feel something.

She was tired and disappointed—and disgusted with herself. She actually fought with her friends over this guy! She was so convinced he was perfect, she hadn't paid any attention to who he really was.

*Just like I did with Brandi,* she thought.

She groaned. *Admit it,* she told herself. *Anna was right about everything! I was starstruck. I let Brandi take over our float because I was impressed with her. Because I wanted to know her rock-star friend.* She had really messed up this time.

At least, she had done one thing right. She had arranged to talk to Josh about their float in the morning. Somehow, he would help her fix things.

*Yeah,* Stephanie told herself, feeling more cheerful. *I did one thing right, after all!*

# CHAPTER
## 13

◆ ◂ ◗ ◆

"Hurry up, you guys," Stephanie called as they raced toward the *Sunshine*. "I can't wait to talk to Josh about our new idea."

She had spoken to Darcy and Allie late the night before, after her date. They had already spoken with Anna and Kayla. Together, they came up with a fantastic new idea for a float.

Their new theme was Romeo and Juliet. They would build a tiny castle balcony, and use the trees and flowers they had already made to decorate the outside.

Stephanie slowed down when she saw that the deck of the *Sunshine* was crammed with small groups of people. They were all talking and whispering to one another.

"I wonder what's going on?" she said.

They climbed aboard and found Darah and Tiffany clinging to each other, crying. Cynthia and Mary were trying to comfort them—as were a couple of kids from other groups.

"Hey!" Josh called, hurrying over to Stephanie. "Did you hear the news?"

"What news?" Stephanie asked.

"Somebody trashed the Flamingoes' float!" he told them.

Stephanie stared at him in surprise. "Trashed their float? When? How? Why would anybody do that?"

"I don't know," Josh replied. "It was a really lousy thing to do. Look, here comes Craig. He knows more about it than anyone else."

Craig's mouth was set in a grim line. He glanced at Stephanie, and the anger in his eyes made her shiver.

"Stephanie," he said, "will you please come to my office?"

"Me?" Stephanie asked. "What for?"

"You'll find out. Now," he repeated.

He strode away. Stephanie stared after him, feeling bewildered. She turned to Josh. He shrugged. He seemed bewildered, too.

"Why would he want to talk to you, Steph?" Kayla asked. Her voice sounded very small.

"I don't know, but I don't have a very good feeling about this," Stephanie replied.

"Well, I'm going with you," Darcy said.

"Me, too," Allie instantly agreed. So did the others. They followed Stephanie off the *Sunshine* and into Craig's office near the marina club-house. Stephanie's stomach was doing nervous flip-flops.

Craig seemed surprised that Stephanie had brought her friends. He stared at them for a long time.

"I suppose you heard that someone destroyed the Flamingoes' float last night," he finally began.

"We just heard," Stephanie said.

"It's the worst thing anyone could have done," Craig said. "It totally goes against the spirit of friendly competition."

He opened his desk drawer and took out a glittering piece of jewelry. He held it up to the light.

"I believe this is yours, Stephanie," he said.

Stephanie took it from him in surprise. "Hey, my ankle bracelet!" she cried. "I wondered what happened to it. Where did you find it?"

Craig folded his hands on the desk. "In the ruins of the Flamingoes' float."

Stephanie's stomach clenched. "How did it get there?"

"You tell me," Craig said.

Stephanie flushed. "You don't think I had anything to do with trashing that float, do you?" She shook her head. "Because I didn't. None of us did."

"Well, Stephanie, that ankle bracelet disagrees with you," Craig told her. "I'm going to bar you from the flotilla."

"B-but that isn't fair!" Stephanie cried. "Can't you see what happened? Somebody found my anklet and put it in their float. They're trying to frame me."

Craig frowned. "I know that you're rivals with the Flamingoes," he said. "And I can't let you get away with this sort of thing."

Darcy frowned. "If Stephanie isn't in, then I'm not in."

"The same for me," Allie declared. Anna and Kayla nodded in agreement.

"Definitely," Anna told him. "We believe Stephanie. She had nothing to do with it."

"All right," Craig said. "I accept your decision. You're all out of the flotilla."

Stephanie stormed out of the office and headed for the parking lot.

"Can you believe Craig?" Darcy fumed. "He didn't even let us defend you, Steph!"

"He already made up his mind," Anna agreed.

"Well, I think he's being totally unfair about the whole thing," Allie said.

"Thanks, you guys. It was great the way you stood up for me," Stephanie told them.

"No way could we be in the flotilla without you," Darcy told her. "We—" She broke off suddenly, staring behind her.

"Well, look who's here," she said. Her voice was cold.

Stephanie turned to see the last human being on earth she wanted to see.

Brandi.

Stephanie glared at her. "Come on, guys, let's get out of here." She turned her back and bent to unlock her bike.

"Stephanie, please wait," Brandi begged. "I need to talk to you!"

"What do you want to talk about?" Stephanie demanded. "The way you and the Flamingoes planted my ankle bracelet in their float?"

"I had nothing to do with that, believe me!" Brandi took a deep breath. "I know a lot of stuff is my fault, but I really had nothing to do with framing you."

"Then you admit I was framed?" Stephanie asked.

"Of course!" Brandi exclaimed. "It was Darah's idea. I didn't believe they were serious at first. It seemed too evil. I really liked Darah and her friends."

"So we know," Anna snapped. "Is that why you gave them the idea for the living garden, too?"

"Look, I don't blame you for hating me," Brandi said. "I didn't know what the Flamingoes were really like. I was just trying to make friends. And then, I don't know, Darah was talking about float ideas, and somehow I just blurted out my living garden idea. And she loved it."

"Why should we believe you?" Stephanie asked.

"Because," Brandi said. "Why would I tell you both the same idea? What would be the point?"

"I don't really know," Stephanie admitted.

"If you're so innocent, why didn't you tell us what happened right away?" Anna asked.

"I tried," Brandi told her. "That's why I was suggesting that you change your float. I didn't want you both to build the same float!"

"Is that really the truth?" Stephanie asked.

"Yes. I didn't know what else to do," Brandi said. "I tried to make Darah switch her float idea, but she wouldn't. That's the reason I stayed in their boathouse so long the other day. I was trying to change her mind."

"We thought you were a traitor," Stephanie admitted.

"I don't blame you," Brandi said. "You must have felt terrible when you saw they had the same float as you."

"We did," Darcy said.

Brandi pushed a stray lock of hair back from her face. "I tried to call you to confess," she told Stephanie. "I figured the best thing was to be honest while there was still time to fix things. But you weren't home last night. So I called Darah and told her what I had done. I thought she'd change her float. Not destroy it!"

"I guess I can understand you getting stuck like that," Stephanie finally said. "But I wish you'd said something a lot sooner."

"I was afraid to," Brandi told her. "I figured you'd be so mad, you'd never be my friend again." She shook her head. "I think Darah was the most upset because you guys did a much better job with your float than they did."

"Why did she think that?" Stephanie asked. "She never saw our float."

"I told her so," Brandi confessed. She paused.

"I thought I heard her say something about trashing their float."

"But why didn't you tell us?" Stephanie asked.

"I wasn't sure what she meant. It didn't make sense then. I didn't realize she was going to frame you. Now I wish I'd been smarter." Brandi hung her head. "I'm really sorry."

"Thanks—for nothing," Anna muttered.

Brandi looked stung. "Maybe there's something I can do to fix things."

"Like what?" Stephanie asked.

"I don't know." Brandi shook her head, then hurried out of the parking lot.

Stephanie watched her go. "I feel sorry for her," she said.

"She cost us a lot of hard work," Anna pointed out.

"And we're out of the flotilla because of her," Darcy added.

"No—because of the Flamingoes," Stephanie said. "It's really their fault."

"We can argue over whose fault it is all we want," Allie said, looking miserable. "It won't change the fact that we're out of the contest."

"You're right." Stephanie felt helpless. "I guess there's no point in any of us hanging around here now."

"If only there were some way we could clear our names," Anna said.

"You mean, if only we could prove that Stephanie wasn't busy trashing the Flamingoes' float last night," Darcy told her.

Stephanie's eyes widened in sudden excitement. She grabbed Darcy by the shoulders. "That's it!" she exclaimed. "Darcy—you are a total genius!"

# CHAPTER
# 14

◆  ◀  ◆  ◆

Darcy stared at Stephanie in amazement. "What? What did I say?" she asked.

"You just gave me the best idea!" Stephanie beamed. "I *can* prove I didn't trash the float last night," she explained. "Lots of people know I wasn't anywhere near here!"

"But you *were* here," Allie pointed out. "You and Zack were rowing at the marina."

"Oh." Stephanie's face fell. Then she brightened again. "Josh!" she exclaimed. "Josh called me at home last night. He knows I was there, and then the guy who rents rowboats can prove that I was here, on the water."

"And your dad can prove when you got home." Darcy looked thoughtful. "Maybe, if you

put it all together, you can show that you never
had time to break into their boathouse."

"I'm sure I can! Let's go see Craig right now,"
Stephanie said.

She had to admit she wasn't thrilled to face
Craig again. It was something she had to do,
though. She ignored the sick feeling in her stomach as they hurried back to the clubhouse and
knocked on Craig's office door.

"What is it?" he called. He looked up in surprise as Stephanie and her friends entered the
room.

"I, uh, I realized I can prove exactly where I
was all last night," Stephanie began. "And that
I couldn't have trashed—"

"That's okay," Craig interrupted with a
slightly shamefaced look. "Josh just came to see
me," he went on. "He told me that he called you
last night and you were home. And that he was
sure you could prove that you weren't at the
Flamingoes' boathouse last night. He also said
you weren't the type to destroy anyone's property, and that he'd quit if I didn't listen."

"Wow," Stephanie said.

Craig grinned. " 'Wow' is right," he agreed. "I
was pretty impressed at the way Josh stuck up
for you. I was on my way to tell you myself. I
owe you—and your friends—a big apology."

"That is so great!" Darcy leaped at Stephanie and nearly smothered her in a giant hug. Everyone started talking at once.

Craig handed Stephanie her ankle bracelet. "I don't know how this got in the Flamingoes' boathouse, but I think you should get the clasp fixed."

Stephanie took a deep breath. "Maybe now you'll believe that the Flamingoes trashed their own float!"

"We *know* they did," Anna added.

Craig coughed, embarrassed. "Well, there's no way to prove that," he said. "But you're back in the flotilla—if you want to be."

Stephanie grinned. "Oh, yes, we want to be. Definitely!"

They hurried out of Craig's office.

"This is so great," Anna said in excitement. "Let's get right back to the boathouse."

"You know, there's more good news, too," Darcy began.

"There is? What?" Stephanie eyed Darcy with interest.

"Well, now we don't need to build a new float," Darcy replied. "The Flamingoes' living garden float is destroyed. So now our float is an original again!"

"Yeah!" Kayla exclaimed.

"That's right!" Anna looked even more excited.

"Hold on," Stephanie told them. "We can't use that float. The Flamingoes will just keep saying that we trashed their float so we could use it."

Kayla looked crushed. "But they're guilty!"

"We can't prove that," Stephanie told her. "Josh convinced Craig that I didn't do it. But nobody proved that the Flamingoes trashed their own float."

"I guess you're right," Kayla said.

"And there's another thing," Stephanie continued. "Craig will probably never try to prove it. The Flamingoes' parents are the richest members of the yacht club, remember?"

"I never thought of that," Allie admitted. She sighed. "Same old story. The Flamingoes get away with everything."

"We'll just have to start over and get going on the design for a totally new float," Stephanie said.

"I bet when the Flamingoes hear that we're building a new float, they'll build a new one, too," Kayla added.

"Who cares what they do?" Anna asked.

They reached their boathouse, unlocked the

door, and hurried inside. Stephanie gazed at their living garden float with a feeling of regret.

"It is too bad we can't use it," she told Anna. "It really does look great."

"At least, we already have an idea for our new float," Anna said. "Juliet's castle, remember?"

"Right!" Stephanie felt a burst of excitement. They were ready to make a comeback.

"Wait!" Allie cut in. "We can't do Juliet's castle! I just realized—Lori McLean's team is doing a palace with a moat."

"Oh, no." Stephanie groaned. "A palace is the same as a castle."

Nobody said anything for a while.

"Come on, guys," Stephanie said. "It's not so bad. We just need another idea."

"We could go back to Anna's original idea," Kayla suggested. "The whale sounded cute."

Anna shook her head. "Even I don't like it anymore. We need more than cute to win this thing. We need something really different. Special."

Someone knocked on the door and pushed it open.

"Brandi!" Stephanie exclaimed in surprise.

"You mean, Spy Brandi," she added with a laugh. "And you're not going to believe what I just did!"

# CHAPTER
# 15

◆ ◂ ◆ ◆

Brandi pulled a mini–tape recorder out of her pocket and held it high. "I got them," she announced. "I got them good!"

"Got who?" Stephanie asked.

"What are you talking about?" Anna demanded.

"The Flamingoes," Brandi declared. "I wanted to prove to you guys that I'm on your side. So I spied on them. They have another really nasty plan in mind. You won't believe it."

"Yes, we will," Stephanie and Darcy said at the same time.

"Let's hear it!" Kayla demanded.

The recorder whined as Brandi rewound the tape and pushed the *Play* button.

They heard Darah's voice first, then all the Flamingoes talking. They were basically trashing everyone they knew.

"Now for the really good stuff," Brandi said.

Darah's voice rang out clearly. "I can't believe that Josh got Stephanie and her lame friends back in the flotilla," she complained. "We've got to find a way to fix them."

"We've already tried just about everything," Tiffany reminded her.

"I have a new idea," Cynthia offered.

Stephanie narrowed her eyes. Cynthia was the smartest of the group. She might actually come up with a good plan.

"Speak," Darah ordered.

"We could drill a hole in their float," Cynthia said.

"That's so simple, it's beautiful!" Darah gloated. "We wait till the night of the flotilla. We sneak into their boathouse, drill a hole, and watch their float sink—in front of the whole marina!"

"What if they keep watch on their boathouse?" Tiffany asked. "How could we drill a hole then?"

"No problem," Darah told her. "If they're hanging around, we just create some distraction.

Some big fuss to get them out of the boathouse long enough for me to sneak in and do the job."

"I can bring in my dad's cordless drill!" Cynthia sounded thrilled.

"But won't they notice the hole?" Brandi asked.

Darah laughed. "Not if I cover it with a piece of tape. Then, when the float is in the water, the tape will get soggy and come off."

"And their float will sink," Tiffany put in.

"Right," Darah confirmed. "Isn't it delicious?"

"Totally humiliating!" Tiffany agreed.

Brandi pressed the Stop button and switched off the tape recorder.

"That's unbelievable!" Stephanie exploded. "I mean, the flotilla will take place in a shallow part of the marina. But there's still a current in the water. How could they even think of sinking our boat! That is so dangerous."

"We could drown," Allie added.

"I can't believe I ever thought they were nice," Brandi said. "They are totally evil."

"They fool lots of people," Stephanie told her.

"But thanks to you, we have proof of how awful they are," Darcy pointed out. "We just play this tape for Craig, and he'll kick the Flamingoes right out of the flotilla."

"Wait," Stephanie said. "There's no point in

going to Craig now. They haven't done anything yet. Darah will just say they were all joking about drilling the hole. He might even believe her."

"I guess that's possible," Anna slowly agreed.

"And besides," Stephanie added with a smile, "telling on them won't be nearly as much fun as turning the tables on them."

"How will we do that?" Allie asked.

"With a decoy. We'll pretend we're still using the living garden float," Stephanie explained. "We'll set it up in one of those old rowboats the marina is going to throw away."

"I get it," Darcy cut in. "The Flamingoes will go after the decoy garden float. They'll drill a hole in the bottom of that boat. Our real boat will be totally safe."

"It's brilliant!" Allie exclaimed.

"But where will we put our real boat?" Kayla asked.

"We could hide it in the weeds under the boathouse," Darcy suggested.

"I love it!" Brandi cried. "The Flamingoes will be so mad when your float *doesn't* sink!"

"You mean *our* float," Stephanie corrected her.

Brandi gazed at her in surprise.

"That's right," Anna agreed. "I think it's time

we made you an official member of our float team."

Brandi's face broke into a huge smile. "Thanks, you guys!"

Allie looked troubled. "What if the Flamingoes tell Craig that we switched the boats? We'll still get in trouble."

"Don't worry," Stephanie said. "They can't tell. They would have to admit they drilled the hole themselves."

"They aren't brave enough to do that," Darcy added. "Those dirty chickens!"

Anna nudged Brandi. The two of them started whispering frantically together.

"What are you guys talking about?" Stephanie asked.

Anna shot Brandi a look of total admiration. "We just came up with the perfect idea for our *new* float!"

"That's right," Brandi agreed. Her eyes sparkled with excitement. "We're going to need feathers," she told them. "Lots and lots of beautiful, fluffy feathers!"

# CHAPTER
# 16

◆ ◀ ◆ ◆

"Can you believe there's only one day until the flotilla?" Stephanie asked.

"Yes," Allie said, "because I'm working so hard." She raised her voice. "Anna, when are we going to get to add the feathers?"

"Soon," Anna promised.

Their new float was starting to look good, Steph thought. Anna and Brandi had really come up with a fabulous idea this time. It was original—and pretty, too.

Stephanie stepped back and stretched. Her muscles ached from sitting in one position.

"Do you think we're going to finish in time?" she asked.

"Absolutely," Anna told her. "Keep working."

Stephanie gazed at the new float in admiration. "I still can't believe that calling the Flamingoes chickens gave you the idea to make this," she said. "A beautiful white swan!"

Darcy lifted a tangled string of tiny white Christmas lights. "Untangling these is my least favorite job," she complained. "My dad makes me do it every Christmas!"

"It will be worth it," Kayla told her. "Those twinkling white lights will look incredible on our white swan."

Stephanie glanced at Anna, who was painting the swan's head. Allie added a last coat of white paint to the swan's cardboard sides.

Even without feathers the swan looked almost real. Stephanie loved the way its wings flared up and back so that the people watching the flotilla would be able to see them riding inside.

"Brandi is a really great designer," Anna told her.

Stephanie turned to look at her friend. "You're amazing, too," she said.

Anna's face lit up. "Thanks. And now I think we're ready to put the feathers on."

"Finally!" Darcy exclaimed. "I can't stand waiting."

Stephanie checked her watch for about the hundredth time. "I can't stand waiting for the

Flamingoes to stage their big distraction. Then we could all stop thinking about that, too."

"I wasn't thinking about it," Brandi admitted.

"I was," Darcy said.

A loud scream echoed through the marina. Stephanie jumped despite herself.

"That must be it!" Stephanie exclaimed. "I thought they'd never get around to it."

They hastily covered the swan with several old sheets. Then they hurried toward the Flamingoes' boathouse.

Another scream split the air. "Sounds like Tiffany," Stephanie remarked.

People came running from all directions as Darah rushed through the wide front doors. "Help, everybody, help!" she shrieked. "Tiffany fell! She's really hurt! Help!"

Stephanie eyed Darah with curiosity. She wondered how Darah liked the new fanny pack strapped around her waist. She grinned. No way could she hide a drill in the skimpy outfits she usually wore!

Darah stared back at Stephanie. "Well, what's the matter with you?" she demanded. "Tiffany fell, and she's hurt! How can you stand there and not try to help?"

"It looks like she has plenty of help already,"

Stephanie pointed out. "We'd just be in the way."

"But she's hurt!" Darah cried. "Don't you care?"

"Of course. We care about anyone who's been hurt," Stephanie told her. She glanced over her shoulder at her friends. "Let's go see how she's doing, guys."

Stephanie pushed into the Flamingoes' boathouse, glancing over her shoulder in time to see Darah racing toward their boathouse.

Everyone was talking at once, but Stephanie could just make out the shrill whine of the drill echoing from their boathouse. She poked Allie in the side. Allie giggled and hid a smile behind her hand.

A few minutes later Darah was back, with a self-satisfied expression on her face.

Tiffany had been lying on the wooden walkway, holding her side and moaning. As soon as she spotted Darah, the moaning stopped.

"Oh, look!" Cynthia cried in a phony voice. "She's much better now!"

Cynthia pretended to help Tiffany stand up. Tiffany gave a weak smile and the crowd started drifting away.

"Oh, Darah," Stephanie called. "Tiffany got better all on her own. She didn't need our help after all."

"Isn't that nice," Darah mumbled. "Well, see you around," she said.

"Definitely," Stephanie told her. "We're not going anyplace."

*Except to our boathouse, to switch the boat with the hole for our real boat!*

"See you at the flotilla!" Kayla waved as they hurried away, trying not to laugh.

"Summer Sailors!" Craig called. "To your floats!"

Stephanie took one more look at the crowded marina. A TV crew was set up by the clubhouse. Newspaper reporters roved through the crowd. Her family sat nearby in the folding chairs that had been set up on the lawn. Other guests lounged on blankets on the grass. The smell of barbecue and popcorn scented the air.

"Isn't this awesome?" Stephanie said to Allie as they hurried toward the boathouse. "There must be three hundred people here!"

"Everyone's having a great time, but I'm too nervous to enjoy myself," Darcy complained.

Stephanie unlocked their boathouse and they rushed inside. It was Kayla and Anna's turn to guard their float. They had taken turns all day to make sure no one got at their *real* float.

"Grab your robes," Brandi called. She had

made them all simple white, hooded robes to wear. Sparkling white sequins trimmed the edges of the hoods and trailed over their shoulders to reflect the twinkling white Christmas lights.

They were dressed in no time. "We looked as if we just walked out of a winter wonderland," Allie remarked.

"Remember to smile. And wave to everybody," Brandi told them as they climbed into their float.

"I wish you were riding with us," Stephanie told her.

Brandi shook her head. "No—you guys deserve all the glory. I'd rather watch, anyway. That way I can be right in the middle of the crowd to hear them cheer for your float!"

An engine purred nearby. The marina's big parasail boat eased into view through the open doors of the boathouse. Stephanie could see Josh at the wheel. Four floats were already hooked up behind him.

"Are you guys ready?" he shouted.

"Ready!" they yelled.

They tossed their tow rope to one of the boys working on the parasail boat. He fastened it and their float lurched once before sliding smoothly out of the boathouse.

# CHAPTER
# 17

◆ ◤ ◆ ◆

Stephanie looked down the line of floats ahead of them. It was a beautiful sight, she thought. The neck of Team One's dragon swayed over the water while the creature scanned the crowd with glowing red eyes.

Allie loved Team Two's rainbow float, with its pot of gold at the end. Lori McLean's castle looked great with rows of brightly colored pennants floating from the top of a tall tower.

Anna giggled at Team Four's float: a great gray whale with a multicolored spout made of shimmering light-sticks.

Stephanie glanced over her shoulder at the Flamingoes' float. They had decided to be water sprites—and call their float a "Water Sprite Garden."

They hadn't used a lot of imagination. She guessed they chose the theme because it was an easy float to make. They simply draped their boat in shiny blue fabric. Their only interest was in the costumes they could wear.

Darah, Tiffany, Cynthia, and Mary wore off-the-shoulder gowns made of shimmering, sheer fabric. They wore glittering gold tiaras and held poles covered with more golden glitter. Glitter also decorated their faces and bare arms and shoulders. They each struck a graceful pose and held it—as if they were statues.

"They look spectacular," Stephanie had to admit.

"Yeah, but their float is nothing," Anna pointed out. "A floating water-sprite garden? It's just the Flamingoes standing in a boat in fancy dresses. Don't make me laugh!"

"They'll never win first prize with that," Allie agreed.

"Tell that to the Flamingoes," Darcy joked. "They always think they only need to show up to win any prize!"

Stephanie glanced at their own float as the flotilla began to move faster. In a moment they'd pull out in full view of the crowd. She wondered how people would react to their swan.

They had worked hard to cover it with soft white feathers. The feathers softened the glow of the twinkling Christmas lights. Stephanie felt as though she were gliding through the water in a cupful of moonlight.

Compared to the brightly colored floats around them, they looked like something out of a fairy tale. They slowly circled the marina, then began another turn.

"Listen!" Darcy suddenly cried.

The crowd onshore was cheering and applauding! Stephanie's heart pounded with pride. Even if they didn't win, just being part of the flotilla was an amazing experience.

Allie nudged her with an elbow. "Take a look at the Flamingoes," she said. "And tell me what's happening!"

The Flamingoes were trying to hold their poses as they whispered to one another. Darah craned her neck, staring hard at Stephanie's float. Tiffany, Cynthia, and Mary also tried to peer into the swan float. All of the Flamingoes were crowding to one side of the boat.

"What are they doing?" Stephanie frowned. "I've got it!" she exclaimed. "They're still waiting for us to sink! They don't know we switched boats."

"You're right!" Darcy started laughing. "They probably can't figure out why the tape hasn't fallen off yet."

"Ha! Let them wonder." Anna waved at the startled Flamingoes and flashed them a big smile.

As they watched, Tiffany dropped her pose and took a few steps toward the end of their rowboat.

The boat began to rock.

Mary shrieked and lurched for the side of the boat to hold on. Cynthia plopped down in the center of the boat.

The boat rocked more. Tiffany lost her balance, her arms flailing. She staggered to one side of the tipsy rowboat.

"Get down, Tiffany!" Darah shrieked. "Are you crazy?"

Tiffany threw Darah a look of panic as the boat teetered crazily.

"Watch out!" Darah shrieked at her. "You idiot!"

Tiffany's side of the boat dipped into the water. Mary screamed.

Cynthia held on for dear life as Tiffany fell backward. *Splash!*

She hit the water shrieking. Darah's eyes widened in shock as Mary and Cynthia slid across the rowboat. The boat filled with water.

*Splash!*

Stephanie gaped in astonishment.

Mary and Cynthia were in the bay.

As if in slow motion, Darah windmilled her arms. For one moment she seemed to hang in midair. Then she kind of flew up and over backward—and landed in the water with her legs kicking up behind her.

There was a shocked moment of silence as everyone in the marina tried to grasp what had happened.

Craig, Ryan, and Jenny ran to help the Flamingoes climb onto the dock.

Stephanie couldn't help it—she burst out laughing. So did Allie, Kayla, Anna, and Darcy. Soon the entire crowd was laughing as the Flamingoes swam for the dock.

Darah was still shrieking. "Tiffany, I'm going to get you for this!"

"It serves them right," Darcy said. "After all the nasty tricks they pulled."

"So much for their first-prize trophy." Stephanie grinned. "Maybe they'll get a special prize—the best swimmers in the flotilla!"

Josh steered his boat to lead the floats up to

the dock also. Everyone tied their floats and climbed out.

Brandi rushed to greet them. "Great flotilla," she said. Her eyes danced with amusement. "I especially loved the Flamingoes' surprise ending!"

"They knew how to go out with a splash," Stephanie joked.

"All I can say is, they got what they deserved," Brandi said.

"All teams to the stage!" Craig called over the loudspeaker. "All teams to the stage!"

Stephanie, her friends, and the other float teams squeezed through the crowd and found places on the stage that was set up near the clubhouse. The Flamingoes climbed up last.

Their glitter makeup was gone. Their hair streamed over their faces. Their beautiful gowns weren't so beautiful anymore. They clung and wrapped around their ankles, making it hard for the girls to walk. They dripped puddles of water.

Craig stared at them, then cleared his throat in embarrassment. "Well, that was an unexpected end to the flotilla," he told the guests. "But still, everybody here worked really hard. No matter who wins first prize, they all deserve a big round of applause. Don't they?"

The crowd whistled and clapped. Stephanie spotted her whole family, laughing and cheering.

"And now for the judges' decision." Craig slid a white envelope out of his pocket and quickly opened it.

Out of the corner of her eye, Stephanie saw Darah and the Flamingoes holding hands.

*I can't believe it! They still expect to win!*

Stephanie actually felt a little sorry for them. Not because their float sank. But because they had absolutely no idea what it meant to work hard enough to deserve a prize.

Craig cleared his throat. "Our grand first place winner is . . . Team Five and its magical swan!"

For a moment Stephanie thought she'd heard wrong. Then her friends started screaming, and she realized it was true. They had won first prize!

They all screamed and hugged and slapped high-fives.

Darah stormed off the stage. The other Flamingoes followed her, dripping more puddles.

Stephanie glanced into the audience. Her dad's smile spread from ear to ear. Joey, Jesse, and Becky whistled and yelled. D.J., Michelle, and the twins jumped up and down. They all looked so proud! She didn't think they could look any prouder if she had won the biggest trophy in the world.

Craig shook each of their hands as he congratulated them. Then he handed them a huge golden trophy. The crowd roared its approval.

"Thank you," Craig said, holding his hands palms out for the applause to stop. "Now I have a surprise for our winners. They also win tickets to the next concert by Zack and the Zees. And here to present them with the tickets is Zack himself!"

Some of the girls in the audience screamed as Zack stepped onto the stage. He smiled at Stephanie. She smiled back.

He looked as cool and cute as ever. But her heart didn't thump and she didn't get a thrill when their hands touched as he handed her the tickets.

"Thanks," she told him. "I bet the concert will be great."

The ceremony ended and Stephanie stole one last look at the floats, still twinkling merrily on the water. She climbed off the stage and headed toward the crowd to join her family.

"Steph!" Zack called. "Steph, wait up!"

He hurried toward her but was stopped by a group of girls asking for his autograph. After signing, he rushed up to Stephanie and grabbed her hand.

"Your float really was awesome," he told her. "I'm glad you won first prize. Why don't we go out to celebrate?"

Stephanie sighed. "Thanks, Zack. But I'm going to celebrate with my friends. You can come along if you like." She hesitated. "But, honestly, I don't think you and I should date anymore."

Zack acted disappointed for a second. Then he smiled. "That's okay. As long as you're still coming to my concert."

"Are you kidding? Me miss a Zack and the Zees concert?" Stephanie pretended to be shocked. "No way! I'm your biggest fan!"

"Great. See you later, then." Zack moved into the crowd to sign more autographs.

Stephanie found herself looking straight into Darah's startled face. Streams of water were running down her cheeks from her drenched hair.

"I guess you want to congratulate me for winning first prize," Stephanie said.

Darah glared. Without a word, she turned and stomped away.

Allie hurried up to Stephanie. "What happened?" she asked.

"Darah just heard Zack ask me out," Stephanie replied. "And she heard me turn him down."

"Things don't get any better than this!" Allie exclaimed. "Our team won first prize, and the Flamingoes were totally humiliated—in public. I can imagine the scene Darah will make about this at the Galaxy Grill."

Stephanie shook her head. "Oh, I'm sure Darah will find some way to blame everything on us," she said.

"And she'll definitely make a big play for Zack, too," Allie pointed out.

"She can have Zack if she wants him," Stephanie said. "If Zack can stand her!"

"Are you disappointed that Zack wasn't your perfect guy?" Allie asked.

"Not really." Stephanie grinned. "Besides— summer isn't over yet!"

Stephanie might still find her dream guy. Meanwhile, there was plenty more sun and sailing. Best of all, she could share the fun—with the most perfect friends in the world!

# FULL HOUSE Stephanie™

| | |
|---|---|
| PHONE CALL FROM A FLAMINGO | 88004-7/$3.99 |
| THE BOY-OH-BOY NEXT DOOR | 88121-3/$3.99 |
| TWIN TROUBLES | 88290-2/$3.99 |
| HIP HOP TILL YOU DROP | 88291-0/$3.99 |
| HERE COMES THE BRAND NEW ME | 89858-2/$3.99 |
| THE SECRET'S OUT | 89859-0/$3.99 |
| DADDY'S NOT-SO-LITTLE GIRL | 89860-4/$3.99 |
| P.S. FRIENDS FOREVER | 89861-2/$3.99 |
| GETTING EVEN WITH THE FLAMINGOES | 52273-6/$3.99 |
| THE DUDE OF MY DREAMS | 52274-4/$3.99 |
| BACK-TO-SCHOOL COOL | 52275-2/$3.99 |
| PICTURE ME FAMOUS | 52276-0/$3.99 |
| TWO-FOR-ONE CHRISTMAS FUN | 53546-3/$3.99 |
| THE BIG FIX-UP MIX-UP | 53547-1/$3.99 |
| TEN WAYS TO WRECK A DATE | 53548-X/$3.99 |
| WISH UPON A VCR | 53549-8/$3.99 |
| DOUBLES OR NOTHING | 56841-8/$3.99 |
| SUGAR AND SPICE ADVICE | 56842-6/$3.99 |
| NEVER TRUST A FLAMINGO | 56843-4/$3.99 |
| THE TRUTH ABOUT BOYS | 00361-5/$3.99 |
| CRAZY ABOUT THE FUTURE | 00362-3/$3.99 |
| MY SECRET ADMIRER | 00363-1/$3.99 |
| BLUE RIBBON CHRISTMAS | 00830-7/$3.99 |
| THE STORY ON OLDER BOYS | 00831-5/$3.99 |
| MY THREE WEEKS AS A SPY | 00832-3/$3.99 |
| NO BUSINESS LIKE SHOW BUSINESS | 01725-X/$3.99 |

**Available from Minstrel® Books Published by Pocket Books**

# FULL HOUSE™
# Michelle

A MINSTREL® BOOK
### Published by Pocket Books

**Simon & Schuster Mail Order Dept. BWB**
**200 Old Tappan Rd., Old Tappan, N.J. 07675**

Please send me the books I have checked above. I am enclosing $_____(please add $0.75 to cover the postage and handling for each order. Please add appropriate sales tax). Send check or money order--no cash or C.O.D.'s please. Allow up to six weeks for delivery. For purchase over $10.00 you may use VISA: card number, expiration date and customer signature must be included.

Name _____

Address _____

City _____  State/Zip _____

VISA Card # _____  Exp.Date _____

Signature _____

1033-26

# FULL HOUSE™
# Club Stephanie

*A brand-new miniseries! Collect all three books.*

*Summer is here and Stephanie is ready for some fun!*

#1 *Fun, Sun, and Flamingoes*

#2 *Fireworks and Flamingoes*

#3 *Flamingo Revenge*

-All Now Available-

*Based on the hit Warner Bros. TV series!*

 A MINSTREL® BOOK

Published by Pocket Books

1357-03

Join the party! Read all about...
# party of five™

# Claudia

◆ *Collect all six books based on the hit TV series* ◆

### WELCOME TO MY WORLD  00676-2/$3.99
What do you do when your family isn't like everyone else's?

### TOO COOL FOR SCHOOL  00677-0/$3.99
Who needs school anyway?

### A BOY FRIEND IS NOT A "BOYFRIEND"  00678-9/$3.99
What happens when your best friend becomes your worst enemy?

### THE BEST THINGS IN LIFE ARE FREE. RIGHT?  00682-7/$3.99
How far would you go to impress your friend?

### YOU CAN'T CHOOSE YOUR FAMILY  01717-9/$3.99
If someone offered you a new life, would you take it?

### THE TROUBLE WITH GUYS  01718-7/$3.99
Is having a boyfriend really the most important thing in the world?

### KEEPING SECRETS  01894-9/$3.99
Why is it so hard to do the right thing?

### MY EX-BEST FRIEND  01895-7/$3.99
What good is a best friend if you can't trust her?

© 1997 Columbia Pictures Television, Inc.  All Rights Reserved.